PUFFIN MODE

The Village
and
Two Village Dinosaurs

Phyllis Arkle was born in Chester and educated first there and then at Liverpool University. Since 1959, she and her late husband have lived in the Thames Valley village of Twyford in Berkshire. She decided to be a writer when at school, but did not begin in earnest until 1960, when she joined a local writers' group and took a course in 'Writing for Children' at Denman College.

Besides writing, she is involved with the Women's Institute movement, and enjoys music (she is a patron of the Henley Symphony Orchestra) and bridge. Her other interests include the history of weathervanes and inn signs, and travelling by Motorail. She loves walking in the Highlands and the Lake District, and has spent many holidays at Sawrey, where Beatrix Potter once lived. Phyllis Arkle is the author of several books for children, including the Railway Cat stories.

Once you have finished reading *The Village Dinosaur* and *Two Village Dinosaurs* you may be interested in reading the Afterword by Chris Powling on page 116.

Other books by Phyllis Arkle

MAGIC AT MIDNIGHT
MAGIC IN THE AIR

THE RAILWAY CAT
THE RAILWAY CAT AND DIGBY
THE RAILWAY CAT AND THE HORSE
THE RAILWAY CAT'S SECRET

THE ADVENTURES OF THE RAILWAY CAT

PHYLLIS ARKLE

The Village Dinosaur
and
Two Village Dinosaurs

PUFFIN BOOKS

PUFFIN BOOKS

Published by the Penguin Group
Penguin Books Ltd, 27 Wrights Lane, London W8 5TZ, England
Penguin Books USA Inc., 375 Hudson Street, New York, New York 10014, USA
Penguin Books Australia Ltd, Ringwood, Victoria, Australia
Penguin Books Canada Ltd, 10 Alcorn Avenue, Toronto, Ontario, Canada M4V 3B2
Penguin Books (NZ) Ltd, 182–190 Wairau Road, Auckland 10, New Zealand

Penguin Books Ltd, Registered Offices: Harmondsworth, Middlesex, England

The Village Dinosaur
First published by Brockhampton Press 1968
Published in Puffin Books 1979
Two Village Dinosaurs
First published by Brockhampton Press 1969
Published in Puffin Books 1981
Published in this edition 1996
1 3 5 7 9 10 8 6 4 2

Typeset by Datix International Limited, Bungay, Suffolk
Set in 12/15 pt Monophoto Bembo

Made and printed in England by Clays Ltd, St Ives plc

Contents

The Village Dinosaur

Contents

CHAPTER I

Discovery in a chalk-pit

"What's going on?"

"Something exciting!"

"Where?"

"Down at the old quarry."

The news flashed through the village and shopkeepers locked up their shops and ran. Housewives rushed out of their houses without even bothering to bolt the doors.

Jed Watkins raced along – as usual, well behind the other boys – down the narrow, muddy, rutted lane leading to the disused chalk-pit. He could smell wood burning. Whatever could have happened? It was at a time like this that he wished he wasn't so much smaller than other boys of his age. He couldn't run as fast and he was always last on the scene.

When, panting, he arrived at the pit, most of the villagers were already there and two cranes were parked nearby. The crowd had made a ring round a bonfire, which shot up sparks, golden against the towering white chalk cliffs. People at the back stood on their toes and stretched their necks to see over or between the heads of those in front.

When he jumped up as high as he could, Jed glimpsed something lying beside the bonfire, something large and mound-like. He ran round trying to find a niche through which he could squeeze his way to the front, but no one would give way an inch. So he tried to make sense out of all the talking and shouting.

A workman from an adjacent building site raised his voice. "Yes, yes, I'm telling you. I drove into the quarry to pick up some rubble and before you could say 'Jack Robinson' the ground gave way. My mate and I managed to jump clear and the lorry disappeared into that large hole over there."

In a voice trembling with excitement, the other man took up the tale. "So we brought the crane and hoisted the lorry up. And it was then we noticed something large and round deep, deep down at the bottom. We lowered ourselves into the hole – we didn't like it a bit, I can tell you – and with our pickaxes we carefully prised it out of a layer of fine red sandstone, just below the chalk level. Then we had to send for another crane, as one wasn't strong enough to haul up this gigantic specimen. We put slings round his body and hooked them on to the cranes.

"And here he is safe and sound on firm ground. Looks to me as though he might revive when he's warmed up."

Jed couldn't stand it any longer. Getting down on all fours and unheeding the protests of a woman who whacked him with her umbrella, and another who trod on his fingers, he pushed his way through the forest of legs. And there, lying beside the bonfire, was the largest and strangest-looking creature Jed had ever seen.

The beast stirred and Jed, watching wide-eyed, shouted, "Look! He's waking up."

The animal slowly lifted up its small head supported on its long neck. Jed could see that a great part of the length of the animal was made up by the very long neck and the very long tapering tail, with a big body in the middle. He let out a whoop.

"It's a dinosaur! It's a dinosaur!" he yelled, throwing out his arms and jumping up and down.

The Parish Clerk, who was standing next to Jed, went pale. "Don't be so ridiculous, Jed," he chided. "There haven't been any dinosaurs on this planet for millions and millions and millions of years."

But Mr Holloway, Jed's headmaster, had managed to make his way through the crowd. "Just a minute," he said, examining the creature. "Jed's right!" he said excitedly. "It *is* a dinosaur! He must have been preserved all this time. He probably got wedged between two rocks and was buried by a sudden sandstorm. There must have been a crack in the layers of rock which have formed on top of him and air has filtered through. All very mysterious, I must say. I've heard of toads and birds – swifts and swallows, and an occasional nightjar – hibernating, but this beats all! We might find an explanation one day." He took a closer look. "He's a young dinosaur by the size of him."

"But he's *huge*, sir, really immense. Much, much bigger than an elephant, and just look at his long, long tail and neck," Jed cried.

"Well he could grow twice as large – up to 80 feet or so long."

"Phew!" said Jed. "We'll call him 'Dino', shall we?" In his own mind Jed had already adopted the creature.

"That sounds a bit obvious, doesn't it?" laughed Mr Holloway. "But it will do for the time being. Yes, let's call him 'Dino'."

"But what on earth are we going to do with him?" asked the Parish Clerk, who was beginning to feel somehow responsible for the strange new member of the community. The crowds pressed back as Dino slowly heaved up his enormous bulk and stood on all fours, his head on its long neck stretching far above the heads of the people. Jed stood his ground and Mr Holloway said reassuringly, "It's all right. He can't bite much with those weak-looking teeth. Just watch out for his tail. He could lash out with that if he felt like it, but I'm sure he's quite docile. He's probably far more wary of us than we are of him."

So Jed put out a trembling hand and actually touched the small horny scales on Dino's right front leg, noticing as he did so that Dino's front legs were shorter than his hind legs – and they were all slightly bandy! Jed's father, Mr Watkins, who stood not far away, looked admiringly at his small son standing beside the great beast.

"Jed always did have a way with animals," he said. And Jed had never felt so pleased and proud. For the first time in his life he didn't mind being small.

"Could I have Dino as a pet?" he asked.

The crowd roared, and Mr Watkins joked, "I'd rather like to see him sitting beside our living-room fire. There'd only be room for his head. And what a head!"

Jed looked up at Dino who was certainly no beauty. In fact, one might say that his rather snake-like head was distinctly ugly. His nose and eyes were on top of his head and his mouth stretched the length of his jaws. But Jed thought he was wonderful.

As warmth seeped through his bones, Dino shook himself and moved his long tail to and fro. The villagers hastily drew back out of reach of Dino's tail, but they shouted encouragingly at him.

Jed called out louder than anyone, "Come on, Dino. Come on. See if you can walk."

The Parish Clerk held up his hand. "We must be practical," he announced solemnly. "Dino has been discovered in our village. Yes, well, all right, within the village boundary – well, *underneath* to be precise – and we'll have to do something about him. Has anybody got any ideas?"

"Could he live on the school playing-field, sir?" suggested Jed, who thought he would be able to keep an eye on Dino there.

But Mr Holloway wouldn't hear of it.

"No, no, no. It takes me all my time keeping you boys interested in your lessons without the added distraction of a dinosaur in the playground."

"Well, what about the recreation ground? That's large enough, surely." The Parish Clerk sounded impatient.

Jed's spirits rose, for Mr Watkins was warden of the recreation ground and Jed lived with his father and mother in a cottage on the grounds, near to the new village hall. Dino would live almost in Jed's own back garden. He could hardly wait for his father's reply.

After giving the matter some thought, Mr Watkins replied, "That's the best idea so far. Dino can sleep alongside the hall. He'll be sheltered there and we'll have to see about getting a load of straw to make a bed for him."

"What about food?" inquired the Parish Clerk. "The village certainly can't afford to keep him. Everybody is still grumbling about the cost of the new hall, let alone having a dinosaur to look after."

Much to Jed's relief, Mr Holloway was ready with an answer. "Dino won't need a tremendous amount of food. He's a plant-eater, not a savage carnivore, so perhaps the farmers would provide a few cabbages and leeks, and other vegetables, to be going on with. The boys can go round collecting leaves and wild plants. We'll have to find out what really suits him."

"Well, for goodness' sake, let's get him to the recreation ground for a start," suggested the Parish Clerk. "We can't stand about here all day. I've got work to do if no one else has." He waved his arms and clucked at Dino, trying to shoo him down the lane towards the village, but the animal appeared quite unconcerned and waited patiently.

Mr Holloway explained. "Dino has got such a small brain, it probably takes some time for an idea to penetrate." He tried giving the animal a light tap on the shoulder with a branch he had picked up off the ground, but all to no avail.

So Jed thought he'd try. Walking away directly in front of Dino, he called over his shoulder, "Good fellow, Dino, come on, follow me!" and whether it was because Jed had a soft, pleasant, persuasive voice, or whether Dino had, from the first, taken a liking to the boy no one ever knew, but, to everyone's amazement, Dino started to move slowly and ponderously down the lane, his large feet making deep holes in the mud.

The Parish Clerk, Mr Holloway and Mr Watkins followed some way behind as they thought it was wise to keep well clear of Dino's long tail. After them came men, women and children with a few dogs joining in to add to the confusion. It was quite a festive occasion and only lacked the village band to make it as good as the Bank Holiday procession.

As they passed through the village Dino occasionally swished his tail and turned his head from side to side. He walked bang in the middle of the road. Oncoming traffic had to pull into one side, and lorries and cars, hooting impatiently, queued behind. And the astonishment on the faces of the motorists! Never before had they seen anyone so small as Jed leading anything as large as Dino. In fact, never before had they encountered anything remotely resembling Dino.

The local woman reporter, who represented a newspaper in a nearby town, happened to be in the village. She whipped a notebook and pencil out of her pocket and, joined by the local photographer, followed the procession.

CHAPTER 2

Dino settles down

Jed turned down the lane leading to the recreation ground and opened wide the double gates at the end.

"Come on, Dino," he urged. "You'll just about manage to squeeze through." But Dino, who, to give him his due, had never seen a gate before, stepped aside and put first one large strong-clawed foot and then another on top of the fence, crushing it like matchwood. The Parish Clerk wrung his hands.

"Oh, dear me, dear me, what *are* we going to do? Dino will ruin us. We'll have to get rid of him somehow!"

"Don't worry, sir. I'll mend the fence," called out Mr Watkins quickly.

Dino obviously recognized shelter when he saw it, for he headed straight for the double glass doors leading into the village hall. He was very surprised when the glass splintered all over his head.

Jed cried out in alarm, "Oh, oh, he'll hurt himself. Come out, Dino."

"He'll be all right," said Mr Holloway. "His hide is thicker than an elephant's."

And sure enough, Dino, looking bewildered, shook the glass from his head like drops of water. He again tried to push his way into the hall, but his neck stuck half-way, so, backing clear, he allowed Jed to lead him to the side of the building.

The Parish Clerk clutched his head in his hands and moaned, "Just look at those plate-glass doors. It will take a lot of ratepayers' money to replace them. Whatever are we going to do?"

Meanwhile, the reporter had been asking questions of everybody and the photographer rushed about viewing Dino from all angles.

Jed's schoolfellows formed an admiring group around Dino, but Mr Holloway called them away.

"Not too many at a time. We don't want to frighten Dino."

Jed had his photograph taken while standing underneath Dino's neck in front of his legs. There was plenty of room and he wasn't in the least afraid.

When he had run out of film the photographer, with

the reporter, rushed off down the lane. The reporter called out. "My word! What a scoop. First in the field all right this time. My editor will be pleased. You'd better look out – all the others will be here soon." She was right. By the time Dino had settled down and had been fussed over by everybody, the "others" arrived. There was a screeching of brakes.

"Look! Here come the television men," shouted the boys, running to meet the two teams who were soon busily unloading equipment and setting it up near Dino's corner. From then on everything was in a state of turmoil. Each team tried to get into the best position for filming Dino, while still more reporters and also many curious sightseers added to the confusion. The centre of all the attraction took little notice of what was going on around him. Squatting on his haunches, he continued sampling the different kinds of vegetables and plants which were offered to him.

Men shouted, pushed and directed and ran about everywhere, over the football pitch and the tennis-courts. One man fell into the paddling pool. The recreation ground, slightly squelchy from recent rain, became a quagmire. No one took any notice of the Parish Clerk who, poor man, was walking round in utter despair.

"We'll never, never, balance the accounts this year after we've repaired all this damage. We'll be ruined, absolutely ruined," he cried to no one in particular, raising his arms skywards. But the excitement and all the hurry and bustle went on around him, and it was getting dark when the filming ceased and the cameramen and reporters dashed back to London. The sightseers then thought about supper and departed with many a backward glance at Dino.

The boys were reluctant to leave and stayed near to Dino with Mr Holloway and Jed's father. The Parish Clerk surveyed the havoc. He shook his clenched fist at a lone cameraman, struggling back to his van.

"How dare you come here without permission . . . and . . . and . . . spoil our ground! Just look at it. Who's going to pay for the repairs, I ask you? Did you think of that?" he shrieked, outraged.

The man looked surprised. "Calm down, guv," he replied. "No one has ever seen a dinosaur before. He'll be a gold-mine if you handle him properly. But you'll have a job keeping him, I can tell you. Everybody will be after him. He'll be on the front pages of all the newspapers and on the television screens too. The film companies will be after him next. There's a fortune to be made out of that animal. He'll be the sensation of the century!"

"*Will* he?" The Parish Clerk looked more kindly at Dino. "Now, I wonder . . .? Jed, give Dino some more food and perhaps he'd prefer milk to drink." He turned to one of the other boys. "Go and see if your father can spare a gallon or two. Tell him we'll pay later."

The Parish Clerk hadn't finished. He paced about and then spread out his arms wide. "I think we'll have to consider building a shelter for Dino here, alongside the hall where there are no windows."

"Can we afford it?" asked Mr Holloway.

The Parish Clerk ignored the interruption.

By now, the other boys had been sent off home. Jed wanted to stay with Dino, but his father said, "No, that won't be necessary. He'll be all right."

Mr Holloway added, "I expect Dino will want to have a good nap – when he's decided he's had enough to eat, that is."

"We couldn't exactly *lose* him, could we?" remarked the Parish Clerk happily.

So Jed went home. His mother had cooked an excellent hot-pot to warm them up, but Jed wasn't hungry. He could talk of nothing else but Dino, until his mother, exasperated, said,

"Now, Jed, up to bed you go, otherwise you'll not be fit for school in the morning. Mind you, I don't think any of us will be good for much tomorrow after today's events! Oh, all right, you can have just one last look at Dino. Put your wellingtons on."

Jed went outside and gazed up at the few clouds scudding across an otherwise starry moonlit sky and looked around at the lighted windows in the houses bordering the ground. He plodded through the mud, enjoying the sucking and plopping noises of each dragging step. As he approached Dino, he saw that the great beast was resting with his head and tail curled round towards his body. Dino raised his head, snuffled a little, and went to sleep again. He didn't object when Jed gave him an approving pat on the top of his head.

Satisfied, and with a warm glow in his heart, Jed made his way back to the cottage and climbed wearily up the stairs. He thought about Dino before he went to sleep and he dreamed about him when he was asleep. In the middle of the night he woke with a start and leapt out of bed and crossed over to the window. He could see the huge elephant-like body of Dino, bathed in moonlight, safe and sound.

It was daylight when Jed woke up again. Jumping out of bed he dashed across to the window. He couldn't believe his eyes. Dino had vanished! Opening the window he peered round, but there was no sign of the animal.

"He's gone! He's disappeared!" wailed Jed, running across the landing into his parents' bedroom.

"Who's gone?" asked Mr Watkins sleepily.

"Dino's not in his corner. I can't see him anywhere."

His father got out of bed. "Get your clothes on," he said urgently. "We'll go and search. He can't have gone very far."

"Oh, dear me," sighed Mrs Watkins, yawning. "Dino's going to be more trouble than a cartload of monkeys."

Jed and his father searched everywhere they could think of and then Mr Watkins sent Jed off to alert Mr Holloway and the Parish Clerk, who very soon joined them in the silent, deserted street.

"He must be somewhere near," said Mr Holloway. "It's extremely unlikely that he's travelled very far – he moves so slowly. But I'll get out my car and we'll scout around the countryside. You'd better come with me, Jed."

So Jed and Mr Holloway got into the car and drove over the river bridge and along the country lanes, keeping a sharp look-out in all directions for a small head on top of a long neck but without success. They returned to the village.

The Parish Clerk was very upset. "Oh, what on earth can we do?" he cried. "We just can't afford to lose Dino. He's going to be such an asset to this village. You don't think he's been stolen, do you?"

"No, I don't," replied Mr Holloway shortly. "And don't forget that yesterday you were wanting to get rid of him."

"Yes, yes, I know, but it's different now."

Suddenly Mr Holloway snapped his fingers. "Did you look in the river?" he asked Jed.

"I searched along the meadows," answered Jed, puzzled.

"No, no, did you look *in* the river?"

"Well , no."

"Oh, for pity's sake, don't say he's been drowned," shouted the Parish Clerk. "Come on, let's go," and they raced through the street again, over the bridge and down on to the river bank. Now, it was only a small river, being a tributary of a much larger river, but it was quite deep in the centre. The surface, rippled by a gentle breeze, glistened in the rays of the early morning sun, and a few swans and ducks could be seen in the distance by the old mill. Suddenly Jed pointed upstream.

"What's that?" he cried.

"It's Dino," said Mr Holloway.

"Where?" asked the Parish Clerk and Mr Watkins.

"Over there," and Mr Holloway pointed out two small ears, two eyes and a nose sticking up out of the water. The eyes had evidently observed Jed, for Dino got up slowly and waded into shallow water. The swans and ducks bounced about on the waves. Jed and his friends all ran to met him.

"Is he all right?" asked the Parish Clerk anxiously.

"Of course he is," replied Mr Holloway impatiently. "Haven't you noticed that his nostrils are placed with his eyes on top of his head? He can breathe and see even though almost completely under the water. That was how dinosaurs used to hide from their enemies." The Parish Clerk was too relieved to bother about Dino's anatomy, and still more relieved when Dino obediently followed Jed back to the recreation ground.

CHAPTER 3

Dino goes for a walk

Dino settled down in his corner contentedly enough and as he had his head well down, Jed was able to talk right into his ear. "I want you to understand that you're quite safe here with us, Dino. We're going to look after you and there's no need to hide away. You've no enemies."

"No natural enemies," agreed Mr Holloway, who had overheard, "but if I'm not mistaken there's more trouble approaching. Come on, Jed, the school bell has rung. We'll have to leave the Parish Clerk and your father to deal with matters. Oh, I realize we haven't had any breakfast," he added, "but we'll have to do without food until lunch-time. You can't expect to lead a normal life when you have a dinosaur on your hands!"

Jed, following Mr Holloway, glanced apprehensively at the two men they passed in the lane, and the Parish Clerk and Mr Watkins greeted the men, both tall and neat and dressed in city-clothes. They were from the Ministry of Health and were very curious about Dino. They started asking questions immediately.

"Quarantine?" repeated the Parish Clerk incredulously. "Put Dino into quarantine? Whatever for?"

"The public has to be protected, and all animals arriving in this country have to go into quarantine for six months," one man explained. "Dino might have cholera, plague or even yellow fever."

"Nonsense!" exploded the Parish Clerk. "And in any case, he hasn't 'arrived in this country'. He's been here all along. Much longer than any of us." (The Parish Clerk laughed at his own joke.) "He's perfectly healthy. Take a look at him."

The advice was unnecessary, for the men couldn't keep their eyes off Dino. "Oh, I grant you he *appears* to be in good condition, but you can't go by that. He'll have to be examined by our vet."

"He's staying right here," replied the Parish Clerk, with a "you-try-and-take-him-away" expression on his face. The two men looked uncertain, and then one of them thought of something. "Well, then, may we inspect your licence?" he asked triumphantly.

The Parish Clerk was very indignant. "Where do I

get a dinosaur licence? Tell me that. Do I have to go to Whitehall for one?" he asked sarcastically.

The men could tell they were making no headway so, with a last look at Dino, they left. "All right. We'll have to see what the Minister of Health has to say about this. You'll be hearing from us," was their parting shot.

The Parish Clerk was fuming. "Think they can take Dino away from us, do they? Well, they can think again. Come on, Mr Watkins, we'd better go and see about those estimates."

Dino watched them out of sight and munched and chewed his food all morning. Then, standing up, he peered over the roof of the hall towards the school. Head on one side, his sharp eyes scanned the landscape. Then he ambled down the lane, this time putting all four feet on top of another section of fencing.

He didn't hurry. There were many interesting things for him to inspect. For instance, at one point over the hedge he saw a row of marrows. He didn't, of course, know they were marrows. To him, they were just delicious-looking morsels. He craned his long neck over the tall hedge and worked his way through the row by taking a bite out of each vegetable.

Just then the Parish Clerk and Mr Watkins came back, closely followed by Jed, out of school now because it was lunch time. The Parish Clerk let out an agonized yell. "Just look at him now! Come away, you great beast! He's eaten all the marrows I was growing for the Horticultural Show. There's not a perfect one left. Oh, oh, I can't stand any more of this. He'll have to go. I've made up my mind."

Jed and Mr Watkins stood helplessly while Dino, alarmed by the Parish Clerk waving his hat at him, set off at a slightly smarter pace towards the village.

"Stop him, Jed! Stop him! Heaven only knows what mischief he'll get up to next," cried the Parish Clerk.

"I'll try, sir" panted Jed, running on ahead. But Dino was evidently enjoying himself and he didn't halt until he reached the ancient inn at the village cross-roads. He could just about see over the rooftop of the two-storeyed inn and gazed at the green fields and, beyond, the river running like a silver thread through the meadows.

The Parish Clerk, breathless, red in the face and with his hat on the back of his head, came up wielding a spanner he had borrowed from the garage farther down the road.

"Oh, don't hit him, please, sir," pleaded Jed.

"Don't worry. It would take more than a blow from this spanner to do much harm, but we've got to turn him back somehow," answered the Parish Clerk, striking Dino smartly across the tail.

But he was mistaken, for Dino moved more quickly than anyone thought possible. As he swung round, his enormous tail lashed against the side wall of the inn. There was a noise like thunder as the bricks and mortar came toppling down. It was just as though a heavy lorry had crashed into the inn and razed one end of it to the ground. The innkeeper and his wife came rushing out into the street and everyone jumped back choking and spluttering. Dino had backed down the road away from the inn. It was not until the dust had cleared a little that they could see exactly what had happened.

"Thousands . . ." muttered the Parish Clerk, his eyes glazed.

"Thousands of what, sir?" asked Jed, anxious to take the Clerk's mind off things.

"Thousands and thousands and thousands of pounds it will cost us before that beast has finished. This settles it. The Ministry of Health can have him – and welcome. I'll inform them straight away. My nerves won't stand any more."

"What's going on?" asked Mr Holloway, who had just arrived.

Jed replied tearfully. "Oh, sir, the Parish Clerk hit Dino across his tail and he swerved right round. He shouldn't be frightened like that."

"Hm, hm, that's interesting," said Mr Holloway. "I imagine it is because Dino has got a sort of nerve centre, which is very important to him, at the base of his spine. It helps him control his very heavy hind legs. We'll have to remember not to alarm him by touching him on the back, unless we really want him to move."

"We won't want him to move," said the Parish Clerk

"And why not?"

"Because he won't be here. I'm going to telephone the Ministry of Health. They can come and fetch him. The sooner the better so far as I'm concerned."

There were murmurs from the crowd, and even the innkeeper, surveying the damage, shook his head in disapproval at the thought of losing Dino. As to Jed, it was almost more than he could bear. He didn't think he could face anyone. Looking at the ground he idly scuffed away at the dust and rubble with the soles of his shoes. Suddenly, he bent down and with his bare hands swept a little pile of rubbish to one side.

"Mr Holloway, sir," he called out, now on his hands and knees. "Come and look at this."

Everybody crowded round and Dino ambled forward, flicked his ears and lowered his head as though he too was anxious to see what Jed had unearthed.

Mr Holloway got out his handkerchief and enthusiastically cleared away more rubble. "I think you've made an important discovery, Jed. I'm sure this is Roman tiling. Look, it's coloured marble, cut and arranged in a pattern. The inn obviously stands on the site of a Roman villa."

He called to the Parish Clerk, who was on his way to the telephone. "It's worth your while coming back to see what I've found."

The Clerk turned back reluctantly. "Well, what is it? A few golden sovereigns?" he asked churlishly. "It will cost more than that to repair the damage caused by this dinosaur."

"Much more valuable than a few sovereigns. There are the foundations of a Roman house under this inn, which means there must have been a settlement here.

Many people will be interested in this discovery. Good old Dino!"

Jed scrubbed away. "Look, sir, here's a piece," he said, pointing at a portion of red marble now clearly visible.

"Looks like a very ordinary bit of tiling to me," muttered the Parish Clerk uncertainly.

"Oh, no, it isn't," said the headmaster. "It's similar to the floors found at the Roman fort further up the river. Dino's stirring things up in this village. And not before time, I might add."

"Can he stay, then, please?" asked Jed quickly.

"Well, er . . . for the time being, anyway," agreed the Clerk. "After all, we can do with more visitors coming to the village. That's always good for trade. Yes, yes, of course he must stay. Just let anyone try taking him away. I'll be ready for them."

Mr Holloway grinned at Jed.

The Parish Clerk turned to the local saddler, whose shop stood opposite the old inn. 'That animal is going to do a lot of good for this village," he announced. "As a matter of interest, I wonder how many hands he is?"

"He's not a horse!" cried the saddler. However, starting at the tip of Dino's tail, he paced slowly along until he came to the animal's outstretched head.

"At a rough guess, I should say he's getting on for 40 feet long, and you can see for yourself how tall he is."

"And he's growing!" groaned the Parish Clerk.

Dino seemed to be getting his bearings, for he turned

round, carefully avoiding scraping the buildings with his tail. Then he slowly made his way back to the recreation ground.

And there was peace and quietness in the village for a time.

CHAPTER 4

Dino raises the alarm

Jed had gone on ahead, and before going back to school, made sure there was a fresh supply of vegetables for Dino. The dinosaur was no trouble at all for the rest of that day. He slept most of the time and ate unhurriedly for almost all the rest of the time. This seemed to be his idea of contentment.

After school, Jed's first thought was of Dino and, joined by several friends, he ran across to the recreation ground. There was a stranger with Dino – a big fat man who puffed away at a cigar. As the boys came running up, he said,

"My, my, you've got an enormous pet here, haven't

you? I'd like to speak to someone about this animal. Who's in charge?" One of the boys went off to fetch the Parish Clerk.

"Good afternoon. What can I do for you?" asked the Clerk politely when he arrived.

"I've come on behalf of the Zoological Society," explained the man. "My committee wish to make an offer for Dino."

"But he's not for sale," replied the Clerk. "We've no intention of selling him. He's the most valuable thing this village has ever possessed."

The man persisted. "Come now, we're much better suited to keep a dinosaur. After all, in a way he's related to the crocodiles and we've several of those reptiles in our zoo. And we've made a special study of diet and ventilation – all that sort of thing. He'll be much better off in captivity."

"Oh, no, he won't," shouted the Parish Clerk. "There's nothing Dino likes better than a stroll now and then." (He didn't think it necessary to enlarge on what had taken place on these excursions.) "And we'd all hate to see him in an enclosure."

The boys added their views.

"Dino will be happy in the village. The Parish Clerk is having a shelter built for him here, alongside the hall."

"And lots of people will be coming to see Dino and examine the Roman remains underneath the inn."

"He's better than a gold-mine."

But the man was determined not to give up easily. "We'll pay you five hundred pounds for him," he said.

"We wouldn't accept five thousand pounds, thank you," replied the Parish Clerk, with just the faintest suggestion of weakening in his voice. "And it's no use trying to bargain with us. We've quite made up our minds."

The man had one last try. "Six thousand pounds," he offered.

After a split second's hesitation, the Parish Clerk bellowed, "No, no, no. We're keeping him for good."

The man shrugged his shoulders. "Well, I hope you won't regret it, that's all I can say. Here's my card in case you should change your mind." He departed.

Dino lowered his head to take another mouthful of cabbage and Jed whispered, "Did you hear? It's all right. No one's going to take you away. The Parish Clerk just said that he's made up his mind you're going to stay with us always."

Jed waited until the Parish Clerk and the boys had left before he too went home for supper.

In the middle of the night Dino woke up. The sky was clear and bright and there was a full moon. He probably felt restless. perhaps he was remembering the Age of Reptiles long ago when, with his fellow dinosaurs, he walked through the swamps and forests. Then, there were no creatures mightier than the dinosaurs.

Dino went down to the river, waded through it and wandered over the cultivated fields on the other side. What a glorious supply of food stretched in orderly rows in front of him. There were hundreds and hundreds of curly kale. He plodded along eating while in his wake appeared deep dinosaur footprints and mangled vegetables.

When he had had his fill, he set off slowly towards the village. He was getting quite good at judging when it was possible to squeeze his huge bulk down a narrow street and he eased his tail gently round corners without knocking into anything. As he moved sedately along the main street, he inspected the shops and houses on each side. It was a warm night and most of the bedroom windows were open. Dino peered into some as he passed. When he came to the Parish Clerk's house he stopped. Who knows? Perhaps he recognized the Clerk, sleeping peacefully in bed? Dino pushed his snout right through the window and gave a loud snort.

This woke up the Parish Clerk's wife, who was lying on the side of the bed nearer to the window. Seeing Dino's eyes – and being half asleep anyway – she let out a mighty shriek.

"Fire! Fire! Fire!" she yelled, throwing off the bedclothes and rushing to the door.

The Parish Clerk woke up with a start.

"Fire?" he shouted. "Where?" and without waiting for an answer, he ran downstairs and dialled "Emergency", shouting down the telephone, "Fire! Parish Clerk's house," before slamming down the receiver.

By the time he had pulled on an overcoat and followed his wife out into the street most of the villagers had been awakened by the eerie sound of the siren splitting the silence. Heads popped out of windows and a few men rushed down into the street.

Jed was out of bed as soon as he heard the siren. He checked that Dino was not in his corner and then, throwing a coat over his shoulders and without waiting for permission, he ran off towards the village. He arrived just as the fire-brigade rolled up, but the sight of Dino unharmed was all that mattered to Jed.

The firemen jumped down from the engine and proceeded to unroll the hoses. The leader called out.

'Where's the fire?"

By this time the Parish Clerk was beginning to feel a little foolish. He began to think there must have been a misunderstanding.

"Well, where *is* the fire?" he shouted at his wife.

She hummed and hawed while the men got more impatient. At last she pointed at Dino.

"Dino?" asked the Clerk disbelievingly. "What's he got to do with it?"

"I think he must have stuck his head through the window and . . . and . . . when I saw his eyes, I thought . . ."

The Parish Clerk couldn't believe his ears, "Mean to tell me we've all been roused in the middle of the night by that animal? Well, this time it's just too much. He'll have to go to the zoo. I'll see about it in the morning. My mind's finally made up."

"Not again!" protested Mr Holloway, who was leaning out of the bedroom window of the schoolhouse opposite. "First Dino's going – then he's staying – then he's going – just like a see-saw."

The Parish Clerk threw up his arms. "Well, you tell me what we're to do with him. I'm tired of hearing how valuable he is. But is he worth it, I ask you? What's he going to get up to next? We'll all be nervous wrecks if we're not going to be able to sleep at night – it's bad enough during the daytime."

The policeman had arrived on his bicycle. "There are enough bogus fire-alarms without an animal joining in the mischief," he said severely.

And the firemen, muttering angrily, were about to leave when Dino lifted up his head and sniffed the air.

Jed looked up at him. "I'm sure Dino can smell something. Yes, yes, now I can smell burning!" he cried.

They all raised their heads and sniffed. Suddenly a figure could be seen rushing down the street towards them. It was Mr Watkins, out of breath and gasping. "There's a fire in the village hall. Hearing the siren, I guessed the fire-brigade would be somewhere down here."

The firemen leapt to their positions, but, unfortunately, they couldn't get past Dino, who nearly filled the width of the street. There was a great hullabaloo as they reversed the machine back the way they had come and took a detour through the narrow back streets. The crowd followed, led by the Parish Clerk and Mr Holloway.

Jed stayed behind with Dino and eventually persuaded him to move. It took them a long time to get home, but Jed didn't mind. He was getting used to the fact that Dino moved so slowly. He waited until the animal, taking advantage of his great height, selected an apple from the top of a tall tree, and again while he nibbled at the green hedges bordering the lane. When they finally arrived at the recreation ground, the fire was well under control.

"What happened?" asked Jed.

"We think the fire started in a waste paper basket," explained his father. "It must have been smouldering for a couple of hours or so before bursting into flames. If it hadn't been for Dino, the hall might have been destroyed. I don't think I would have awakened if I hadn't heard the siren."

"Dino is a real treasure in more ways than one," said the Parish Clerk approvingly.

"Oh, here we go again," said Mr Holloway. "I suppose we're keeping him now?"

"Of course he's staying with us," said the Clerk. He glanced at Dino. "Look at those water plants clinging to his hide. He's evidently been in the water again. Seems to like it. Do you think it would be a good idea to dig a pool for him?"

"Well, it will cost quite a bit, but if the ratepayers are prepared to subsidize it, I don't see why not," agreed Mr Holloway.

"He's worth his weight in gold to us, is Dino," said the Clerk.

Jed went back to bed feeling more contented. It

would certainly appear that Dino was going to be allowed to stay with them, but he wished the Parish Clerk wouldn't keep changing his mind. After all, Dino couldn't be expected to stay quietly in his corner, day and night, could he? A growing dinosaur needed exercise.

CHAPTER 5

Dino puts his foot in it

While the villagers were getting used to having a dinosaur among them, Jed thought that only his father understood exactly how much Dino meant to him now. The Parish Clerk had been busy getting the estimates for the building of a shelter, and also for a pool. He was not at all worried about the cost.

"You'll see," he would say cheerfully, "before very long Dino will put this village on the map. We'll be famous."

It was true that there was no lack of interest in Dino and in the old inn. Archaeologists had been busy carefully removing some of the tiles which Dino had exposed, and taking them away for examination to the museum in the nearby town. In fact, everybody seemed happy – not least Dino, who still spent his days chewing and sleeping and occasionally taking a stately saunter.

Jed had almost got over his fear that he would lose Dino, when one day another stranger appeared. Jed was feeding Dino at the time and the man, tall and thin, smartly dressed and with a shrewd face, stood a few paces away. He took a good look at Dino and Jed, who was always close to Dino when danger threatened. They made a strange couple – rather like a lion and a mouse together.

The man came up to Jed. "Who owns this animal?" he asked.

"Why, we do, of course."

"Who are 'we'?"

"All of us, the Parish Clerk and the villagers and . . . and . . . me, sir."

"Well, will you please go and tell the Parish Clerk that I'd like a word with him?"

So Jed, with a worried frown on his face, ran off to the village and soon returned accompanied by the Clerk.

"Now what's all this?" asked the Clerk. "Who owns Dino? Hasn't Jed told you? We own him, of course, and, what's more, no one's going to take him away."

"Perhaps you'll listen to what I've got to say first," replied the man. 'I'm the director of a film company and they would like to buy this dinosaur. Never before in our wildest dreams did we think we'd have the opportunity of owning a dinosaur."

"True – you're not going to have the chance. He's not for sale." The Parish Clerk's voice was firm.

"We'll give a good price for him," said the director.

"Not interested. In any case we've already been offered six thousand pounds for him."

"Ten thousand pounds, then," said the man quietly.

The Parish Clerk wavered, but then he noticed Jed's stricken face and being at heart a kindly man – and also an honest one – he said, "Still not interested. He's not mine to sell. He belongs to the whole village and perhaps, especially to Jed, here." Jed straightened his back with pride and relief and gave Dino another cabbage.

The man knew he was defeated. "All right. I can tell you're determined not to bargain with me, but would you consider loaning him to us for, say, a week or two? We could do some good filming in that time. And the boy could come along as well. We could use him in the crowd scenes."

The Parish Clerk thought about this. "We'll see," he replied. "I'll have to put the matter before my council, and Jed's father would have to give his consent. I'll let you know our decision if you care to get in touch with me again. But it couldn't be for some time yet, as Dino has got to become really acclimatized here first."

"I'll certainly come over again," said the man without hesitation.

When he had gone the Parish Clerk turned to Jed.

"You know, he's got a point," he mused. "To whom does Dino really belong? I trust we have the right to keep him."

Jed fervently hoped so. He had thought everything was going to be quite all right, but the Parish Clerk's words had put fear back into his heart.

Dino was very good for a day or so. Now and then he wandered round the recreation ground watching the children at play. Sometimes he went as far as the gate and seemed to be watching for Jed coming down the lane. Soon he'll know exactly what time I'm due home, thought Jed happily. He's better than any dog!

But one day Dino went off to do some more exploring. It was lunch-time and the few people in the street stood to one side and smiled at Dino. He was doing no damage and they didn't attempt to stop him. He treated himself to a leaf from one tree and a soft apple or two from another and even helped himself to a cauliflower from the open stall outside the greengrocer's shop.

Leaving the village behind, he came across an open space where the foundations for twelve new houses on an estate were being laid. The builders, having finished their picnic lunch, were resting under a tree reading newspapers. They didn't glance up.

Dino plodded slowly across the foundations, until at one point the ground started to give way. As he moved forward, he sank down deeper and deeper and deeper until his legs were completely submerged. Just then one of the men glanced up.

"Hey, look!" he yelled at the top of his voice, "Dino's disappearing into the ground again!"

They all leaped up and ran across. Dino was by now up to the top of his back in rubble. Only his head and neck were showing. Poor Dino! He was quite incapable of climbing out of the hole.

"Get the cranes – and the slings," ordered the foreman. "Good heavens! Pulling Dino out of craters is becoming a habit. And just look at the mess."

With a great deal of effort and many encouraging shouts they eased him out. The Parish Clerk came running up just as Dino surfaced. He was speechless with wrath and amazement until Jed and Mr Holloway and some of the boys came along, when he found his voice.

"Look at that damage!" he croaked.

Mr Holloway spoke up. "I told you all along that there was a stream running under this field. Many a time as a boy have I lain down, put my ear to the ground and listened to the water gurgling away. But no, oh, dear me, no, you wouldn't listen to me."

The Parish Clerk ignored him. "More expense. I don't know what we're going to do . . ." he groaned.

"'Dino will have to go,'" quoted the headmaster.

"Who said he'd have to go?" asked the Parish Clerk sharply.

'Oh, I thought *you* were going to say it again," replied Mr Holloway mildly, winking at Jed.

"If anyone tries to take Dino away from this village, they'll have to reckon with me," said the Parish Clerk.

"But, really, I don't know whether he's going to be worth it." Off he strode, shaking his head, to fetch the architect.

By the time he arrived back Dino was once more on firm ground. He shook his head in bewildered fashion and swished his tail rather menacingly.

The architect inspected the ruined foundations and turned to the Parish Clerk. "Well, well, well. Dino has certainly done us a good turn," he said. "There is an underground stream below this field –"

("I told you so," said Mr Holloway to the Parish Clerk.)

" – and if Dino hadn't gone through like this, the houses might have collapsed one day."

"But surely you tested the ground first?" grumbled the Parish Clerk.

"Yes, yes, of course, but the usual borings couldn't have reached as far down as the stream. The houses might have been quite safe, but on the other hand they might not. It's just as well Dino has discovered the weakness. He's a great animal, that dinosaur."

"I can see I'm going to have a stormy council meeting tonight," said the Clerk, "But I'm standing by Dino. He's worth every penny he costs us. I've been thinking, Jed, he hasn't got a proper drinking trough, has he? I'll order a stone horse-trough for him"

"Excellent," agreed Mr Holloway. "To be paid for out of the rates?"

Dino had wandered off and Jed discovered him sitting on his haunches by the hole in the chalk-pit.

"Come on, Dino, time to go back," he said. Dino, with a backward glance down the hole, moved away.

Jed made a fuss of him and, when the small snake-like head was on a level with his own, told him, "You're going to have a stone drinking trough, just like the ones horses use. And the Parish Clerk is *quite certain* – well, I *think* he is, I *hope* he is – you're going to stay with us for ever and ever. You're such a clever animal!"

CHAPTER 6

Dino gets on the line

Jed slept much better at night, now that he felt assured Dino was going to stay with them. One morning, however he woke up and discovered that Dino was missing again. He wasn't unduly alarmed. And not until he had gone out and searched everywhere – not forgetting to look in the river this time – did he begin to panic. He ran along to the Parish Clerk's house and knocked on the door. The Clerk popped his head out of the bedroom window.

"Missing? Not again!" he sighed. "Oh, that beast. Why ever did I say that we'd keep him? There's no peace now. Ah, well, wait there, Jed. I'll be down soon."

As he stepped into the street, the postman came along and, with a cheery, "Good morning," handed the Parish Clerk a bundle of letters.

"Have you seen Dino anywhere?" asked the Clerk. "No? Well, we'll have to go and search, I suppose. No time for these now," and he went back into the house and put the bundle of letters on the hall table. As he was turning away, he picked up one of the letters. "Half a minute, Jed. This one looks important," he said.

Opening the letter, he read it and then called out excitedly, "Why, Jed, this is from the Minister of Health. He advises me that after consultation the government has decided that Dino belongs to us. He will be our sole responsibility. Come on, Jed, we've got to find that animal. Go and tell Mr Holloway he's missing again."

In spite of his anxiety, Jed heaved a huge sigh of relief as he hurried across the road to the schoolhouse and roused Mr Holloway, who soon joined them.

"But you *can't* have looked everywhere," he said. "Not in the river? Nor by the hole in the old quarry? Dino has a habit of sitting there."

Mr Holloway thought for a few minutes and then cried, "Dash it all. Why didn't I think of it before? Remember the circus which passed through the village yesterday? I'll wager anything they've enticed Dino away. Come on, we'll get the car and go after him."

Fortunately it was a Saturday, so there was no school to worry about. They climbed into the car and it seemed ages before they neared the outskirts of the town. They could see in the distance the flag on the big top. Jed, sitting tense on the back seat, leaned forward and peered between the heads of the Parish Clerk and Mr Holloway.

Then, "There he is, there he is, over there!" he shouted, quite unnecessarily for both Mr Holloway and the Parish Clerk had caught a glimpse of the unmistakable small head at the end of the long neck. Mr Holloway stepped on the accelerator. As they passed through the gates into the field they could hear the roaring of lions and the chattering of monkeys and noises from other animals coming from the direction of the menagerie.

They parked the car and rushed off towards Dino who, as usual, was surrounded by an admiring though somewhat awe-struck group. Dino lowered his head, as he often did now when Jed approached, and Jed, his heart nearly bursting, gently pulled at his ears. He couldn't imagine how he could ever live without Dino now.

The Parish Clerk sent someone off to find the proprietor, who soon came bustling through the noisy crowd. When he could make himself heard, he was most apologetic.

"Yes, I'm really sorry about this. You see, two of my men spotted Dino as we passed through your village yesterday and, without a word to me, they went over last night and brought him here. Took them a long time. He's a slow mover, isn't he? My men didn't realize he belongs to you. They thought he'd cause a sensation in our circus. I was going to bring the animal back later today."

The Parish Clerk produced the letter from the Minister of Health. The man agreed, "Yes, of course, I realize we have no claim on Dino. But would you consider selling him to us?"

The Parish Clerk's voice rang out. "No, we wouldn't dream of selling Dino. He's ours for good."

Jed pressed his fingers into Dino's neck and whispered, "Hear that?"

They started the slow journey back to the village. Jed walked in front of Dino, and Mr Holloway and the Parish Clerk followed in the car. Boys and girls kept pace with them while traffic queued up behind him. Mr Holloway leaned his head out of the car window.

"Turn left at the cross-roads, for goodness' sake, Jed," he called out. "Go down the old road."

They soon left the town behind and the children regretfully turned back and went home. There was very little traffic on the minor road, which was just as well for Dino liked to stop now and then.

On one occasion they had a long wait while he slowly stripped all the leaves off a sapling. Then, just when they thought he was ready to go on again, he took it into his head to wander off the road, through a thicket, crushing young trees and shrubs as he went, and on to the adjoining railway line. As usual he left a stretch of crumpled fence behind him. He took no notice of the Parish Clerk's frenzied attempts to stop him as he ambled along the line.

"Oh, oh, more expense!" screamed the Clerk. "The railway will make us pay for new fence and also fine us for trespassing. Where's the money coming from? He'll have to –"

"Don't say it," said Mr Holloway, exasperated. "I'm tired of hearing you say, 'He's got to go – He's staying – We can't afford to keep him – No one's going to take him away from us.' You'll have to make up your mind about it. He belongs to us and he's staying. No matter what the cost."

The Parish Clerk opened his mouth. "Don't argue," ordered Mr Holloway. He looked at his watch. "Dino is on the Up line and it's half past eleven. The express will be along any minute. Jed, run along to the signal-box and alert the signalman. Quick as you can and we'll try to get Dino off the track."

Jed raced along the top of the railway embankment as fast as his short legs would carry him. In spite of the efforts of the Parish Clerk and Mr Holloway, Dino loped along the line and, surprisingly, kept pace with Jed. He turned, gasping, and tried to wave Dino back, but still on he came. Jed climbed up the steps of the signal-box. The signalman was very surprised.

"A dinosaur – on the line? Blimey, I've had cows on the line, but never a dinosaur before." He slammed levers hard over to reverse the signals to danger and then started back as Dino tried to push his head through the open window of the box.

"Goodness!" marvelled the signalman. "There could have been a nasty accident, but I don't know who would have had the worst of it, Dino or the train!"

The train could now be seen in the distance and as it approached the "home" signal, its brakes were rapidly applied and it screeched to a stand. The driver jumped down from his cab and came along the line. He stopped to examine something as he neared the signal-box.

Giving Dino a very surprised look, he called up to the signalman, "What a mercy you were able to halt the train before it struck that telephone cable lying across the line."

"What cable?" asked the signalman, mystified.

"Why, didn't you know about it? There, just in front of my train. I only missed it by a few inches. The police will have to get busy. I expect this is the work of mischievous boys. Pity they don't realize how many lives are at stake when they behave in this irresponsible manner."

"I stopped the train because Dino was on the line," explained the signalman.

Mr Holloway and the Parish Clerk came running up. "Dino has done it again," cried Jed. "He's saved the express from being derailed."

Passengers were leaning out of the windows all along the train. They had read about Dino in the newspaper and had seen the pictures of him on television, but to view a live dinosaur at such close quarters was something they wouldn't have missed for anything.

Dino started to move forward, and for one awful moment Jed thought he was going to try and push the train back along the line, but he turned when Jed ran in front of him. Eventually they managed to get Dino through the thicket and back on to the road again. The passengers cheered and waved as the train drew away. The signalman called out.

"Don't concern yourselves about the damaged fence. We'll soon put that right."

"Clever Dino," laughed the Parish Clerk.

"'We wouldn't part with him for anything!'" said Mr Holloway, with a sidelong glance at Jed.

"No, no, of course not," agreed the Parish Clerk innocently. "I noticed yesterday Dino ate some bread put out for him. I think I'll order a dozen loaves a day for him. We must pamper him a little. He's so helpful!"

"Who's going to pay the baker for the bread?" asked Mr Holloway.

"Oh, really, what a silly question," replied the Clerk.

As they neared the village, Dino insisted on turning down the lane leading to the old chalk-pit. He walked in a leisurely manner into the quarry and stood for a time looking down intently into the hole. They led him away, but as they were going back up the lane, they heard a crash behind them.

They turned and rushed back. Dino followed them. Hard on their heels came the workmen from the building site. They all gazed down into the hole which had appeared alongside the one already there. There was an awed silence, then,

"Do you see what I think I see?" whispered one of the men.

Mr Holloway knelt down and looked into the hole. He said solemnly, "I should say there's another dinosaur down there!"

The Parish Clerk couldn't believe it. "*Another*? Another dinosaur?" he wailed. "Just when I'd become reconciled to owning one dinosaur, but two . . ." He spread out his hands in despair. "Two of that *size*, I ask you . . ."

"It will mean twice as much interest in our village," smiled Mr Holloway.

"And twice as much expense," moaned the Clerk. "I won't be able to stand it. He'll have to –"

"Oh, no, no, no, he won't have to go," put in Mr Holloway quickly. "It has already been decided that Dino belongs to us, so I don't see how we can get out of adopting his twin as well, even if we wanted to, do you?"

"Go and get the cranes," ordered the foreman. "We're becoming used to this," he added in a resigned tone of voice.

Jed, tense with excitement, watched the new arrival being hoisted out of the hole. This dinosaur was smaller than Dino. Had Dino grown with all the food and milk he'd been having, wondered Jed. Or was this a younger animal?

Jed whispered to Dino, who had his head well

down, "Hasn't it been a wonderful day? We've been told officially that you belong to us. And now you've got a playmate."

Jed helped to gather wood to make a bonfire and soon the newcomer woke up and rose to his feet, just as Dino had done not so long before. News had spread round the village and a crowd soon gathered. People laughed and shouted as Dino's twin reared his head on the long, long neck and looked down at them.

"Well, Jed, what shall we call this one?" asked Mr Holloway.

" 'Sauro', sir," said Jed promptly.

"Sauro?"

"Yes. *Dino* . . . and . . . *Saur*–o."

"Ha, ha, what do you think of that for a name, Mr Parish Clerk?" asked Mr Holloway. But the Parish Clerk, poor man, was in too much of a daze to understand properly what was being said to him.

"Two," he kept repeating to himself. "I was just about getting used to managing one, *but two* dinosaurs . . . This village will never be the same again!"

Two Village Dinosaurs

Contents

CHAPTER I

A companion for Dino

Fancy finding *another* dinosaur hibernating in the old chalk-pit – a companion for Dino! Jed Watkins couldn't get over it. Using two cranes and slings, workmen had managed to lift this colossal animal out of the layer of fine sandstone in which it had lain for millions and millions and millions of years. Jed had immediately named this animal "Sauro".

Jed looked round at his father, warden of the village recreation ground, who was standing among the crowd of villagers.

"Look, Father!" he shouted, his voice shrill with excitement. "Sauro is smaller than Dino, but I bet you could drive a tractor between his bandy legs without actually touching him."

"A small tractor, perhaps," Mr Watkins agreed smiling.

Sauro, warming up by a bonfire, shook himself and rose slowly to his feet. Dino moved forward and Sauro seemed delighted to see him. Their great long necks swayed to and fro above the crowd and they prodded each other with their small snake-like heads. The sudden noise of aircraft flying low overhead did not disturb Dino, but Sauro raised his head and probed the air at this unknown danger. His muscles rippled under the hide and his tail twitched nervously.

"Will he be all right, sir?" asked Jed anxiously, turning to Mr Holloway, his headmaster.

"Oh, yes, yes, I'm sure he'll soon settle down. Animals are just like people. They don't take to change at first. Give him time. Remember a modern world must be a confusing and frightening place for a dinosaur."

The Parish Clerk was standing near Jed. His face wore a solemn, worried look. He'd grown quite fond of Dino, but the thought of having to put up with the antics of yet another dinosaur was upsetting.

He called out to the laughing, jubilant crowd. "It's all very well, but have you thought of the extra food needed – to say nothing of shelter for the winter? And if this one is anything like Dino, there'll be trouble sooner or later, mark my words!"

The villagers paid no heed to him.

"You'll see!" he shouted. "Anyway, we'd better get

them along to the recreation ground. Some people seem to have nothing to do and all day to do it in. Lead the way, Jed. Dino will follow and let's hope Sauro will take the hint."

Jed walked on ahead, whistling. Dino raised his head and listened. After allowing time for the order to sink in, he followed meekly after Jed. Sauro, long, tapering, whip-lash tail churning the mud, also moved forward very, very slowly. The Parish Clerk, Mr Holloway and Jed's father kept pace with Jed. The villagers followed the dinosaurs, keeping well away from Sauro's well-armed feet and tail. They knew it would take time before the new arrival trusted humans and became reliable. It was a very long procession.

People who had been unable to go to the chalk-pit leaned out of windows along the street. One or two waved flags. Some made do with dusters. They called to one another.

"We'll have the television people here again."

"And the reporters."

"And the press photographers."

"Isn't it fun!"

But the Parish Clerk didn't think it was so funny. "You'll soon stop laughing when you're told there'll have to be an extra penny on the rates, 'for the upkeep of dinosaurs'. I know you ratepayers!" he cried.

Sauro, ambling along behind Dino, peered over hedges and walls. Then, something attracted his attention. Unfortunately, it happened to be the rose-bed in the garden at the side of the Parish Clerk's house.

Everybody was forced to halt. People a long way off in the rear of the procession craned their necks, wondering what had happened.

Sauro swung his long supple neck over the hedge, bent his head and slowly sniffed at the roses. His soft teeth pulled at a beautiful yellow rose, which slowly disappeared into his mouth. Then, carefully avoiding the thorns, he took another and yet another.

"Food is the first thing an animal needs," observed Mr Holloway.

But the Parish Clerk was very put out. "Oh, what a calamity! Dino ate all my prize marrows and now Sauro's going for my roses. I'll have nothing, absolutely nothing, to exhibit at the shows. And all because of these two dratted dinosaurs. How I wish I'd never set eyes on either of them!"

Mr Holloway chuckled. "Things will liven up enormously now we have *two* dinosaurs. We must expect a few casualties here and there. Such is the price of fame!"

"Wait until Sauro gets at your delphiniums. You won't be so pleased then," retorted the Parish Clerk.

"Oh, but he won't bother with my delphiniums. Once he's developed a taste for roses, he'll stop at nothing to get at them."

"Sauro will soon learn to behave, sir," called out Jed, anxious to keep the peace. "Dino doesn't steal much now he's got used to his vegetables."

Jed ran on ahead. "Come on, chaps, nearly there," he encouraged, whistling furiously. Sauro reluctantly withdrew his long neck and followed Jed and Dino down the lane.

"Watch out for the fence, Jed! We've only just repaired it after Dino's efforts," bawled the Parish Clerk.

But it was too late. Dino stepped gently through a gap in the fence like an elephant that has learned to use its feet carefully, but Sauro trampled on the fence and crushed it into the mud.

The Parish Clerk covered his eyes with his hands and Mr Holloway said, "It's no use, Mr Parish Clerk. We'll have to take down this section of fencing altogether for a time, otherwise we'll be putting it up, taking it down, putting it up again – it's not worth the trouble."

The Parish Clerk groaned. In fact, he'd done a lot of groaning ever since Dino had first been dug up out of the pit. No one took much notice of him now. "If only we could get rid of them both, I'd be a much happier man," he muttered.

Mr Holloway spoke firmly. "You know you don't really mean that. Dino belongs to us and now we have Sauro as well. They're both ours."

"He'll be no trouble at all, sir," said Jed optimistically.

"No trouble!" echoed the Clerk, thinking of Dino's frequent, usually disastrous, outings.

"No trouble at all," repeated Mr Holloway confidently. "Moreover, we must get ready for a greater interest in our village. Never fear, Dino and Sauro will pay for their keep."

"I hope you're right," exclaimed the Parish Clerk.

Dino made his way to the side of the new hall where food and drink were laid out for him. Sauro followed, rubbing shoulders with his companion. He sniffed at the food uncertainly. Jed picked up a large cabbage and, pulling it apart, offered a few juicy leaves to the dinosaur. Sauro slowly sucked them into his mouth and began munching. He evidently liked the taste for he took some more. When he had finished, he lowered his head to the stone horse trough and noisily took a long drink.

"Teaching an animal to eat food he's not used to needs a lot of patience. That's where you will come in, Jed," said Mr Holloway.

"I hope Jed will be able to persuade Sauro to leave my roses alone," said the Clerk. "And, another thing, the milk will cost far too much. We just can't afford it."

"Oh, Dino drinks very little milk now, sir. I've been adding more and more water to his diet. And I'll take them into the lanes so that Sauro can eat dog-roses." Jed was determined to put the Parish Clerk's mind at rest.

"That's the idea," said Mr Holloway approvingly. "Don't start Sauro on milk. What he never knows, he'll never miss. They'll both thrive on water. And make sure Sauro eats some honeysuckle as well as dog-roses. Keep him sweet!"

Jed's schoolfriends were rushing about gleefully. Not another village in the whole world owned one dinosaur, let alone two. Suddenly, one of the boys pointed down the lane and shouted "Here they come!"

The Parish Clerk shuddered when he saw the television vans turning into the lane. News certainly travels fast. There was no peace nowadays. And why, oh why, had it rained last night, making the ground so wet and soggy underfoot? He was thinking back to the day Dino had arrived. The hubbub . . . reporters and photographers rushing about . . . cables trailing . . . grass trodden down . . . mud everywhere . . . the paddling pool a dirty brown colour!

It was happening again and he couldn't bear it! Despairingly, he turned towards the village hall. He went through the open double glass doors and sat down heavily on a hard wooden chair. then he put his head in his hands and waited until it was all over!

CHAPTER 2

The Best-Kept Village competition

Jed stayed close to his two charges as the reporters and photographers – and the villagers – crowded round. Such a commotion had never before been heard in the village, not even when Dino had arrived. There was more noise than when the annual fête was being held on the recreation ground. It was getting very late when the last van bumped down the lane and everyone, tired out, decided to go home. Jed was left with his father and Mr Holloway.

"You'd better go and tell the Parish Clerk it's all clear, Jed," suggested Mr Holloway. So Jed went into the hall and tapped the Parish Clerk on the shoulder.

"They've gone, sir," he said timidly.

The Clerk was still in a stupor. He got up slowly and went and stood outside the hall. His eyes, missing nothing, roved all over the recreation ground and then rested finally on Dino and Sauro. "Still eating, I see. Their jaws never stop working!" he said indignantly. "And just look at this ground!"

"The dinosaurs have to eat a lot to keep their enormous bodies healthy," said Mr Holloway reasonably. "And don't bother your head about the ground, Mr Parish Clerk. It won't take long to get it really shipshape again."

But the Parish Clerk wouldn't be pacified. "I'll tell you something," he said. "We won't get any further in the Best-Kept Village competition. The judges will be visiting us again any day now. And to *think* we were in the 'possibles' list for the first time. I had high hopes of reaching the finals." He sighed. "But look at this ground – never seen anything like it in all my life. And think of my garden . . ."

"Don't worry," said Mr Holloway again. "First thing in the morning, I'll go along to the nurseries and buy some flowering rose-bushes in containers to replant in your garden."

"And I'll tidy up this ground so that you won't recognize it," promised Mr Watkins.

"Oh, and I'll do anything, *anything at all*, to help, sir," offered Jed eagerly.

Mr Holloway and the Parish Clerk went home and

Jed, helped by his father, made sure Dino and Sauro were comfortable. Mr Watkins had to laugh as he watched his small son's figure disappearing from view as Jed walked round the great squatting beasts. The dinosaurs certainly took up a considerable amount of room!

"Hurry up, Jed. It's getting very late. High time you were in bed," Mr Watkins called out as he walked off across the ground to the cottage.

"Won't be long," answered Jed. Sauro's hide looked dried-up and dusty, the result of long hibernation. Never mind, Jed knew that dinosaurs liked, more than anything, to be in water. Dino had got into the habit of bathing daily in the river and, no doubt, Sauro would do the same. Jed wasn't worried. Sauro would be all right.

He gave the animals a last look-over before running off home, thinking how lucky he was to live right on the recreation ground, so near to where the dinosaurs were quartered.

Jed went willingly to bed. When he crept out early next morning and stole a look through the window, there was no sign of the animals. He dressed very quickly and was out of the house before his parents had awakened. He ran through the village, over the bridge and down on to the river bank, laughing out loud when he saw four ears sticking up out of the water like submarine periscopes. Several ducks, tails flapping, were keeping well out of the way.

"Out you come, Dino, and you too, Sauro," he

ordered. He whistled and waited. He was used to waiting. Eventually, Dino's neck rose up slowly like a conning tower and Sauro's followed. Their tails floated on the top of the water as they walked towards the bank. Dino lowered his head for Jed to tickle behind his ears. One day Sauro will do the same thing, thought Jed, looking fondly at the two great beasts lumbering out of the water.

The village was already stirring as Jed led the animals back through the street. Any day now the judges would be coming for the second time to inspect the village for the Best-Kept Village competition. There had been great activity during the past few weeks. Gardens and grass verges had been tidied and window boxes replanted. Some shop-fronts had been repainted, the war memorial had been scoured and all the inn signs had been cleaned.

The Parish Clerk, like a general in command, stood on his front doorstep, looking sharply up and down the street for the least trace of litter or untidiness. Jed wished Dino and Sauro would hurry. Their large bodies nearly filled the street and their heads reached over the rooftops. They ambled along at snail's pace. When the Parish Clerk saw them, he ran forward waving his arms and shouting, "Get those beasts back to the recreation ground, Jed."

As they drew nearer, he grew more agitated. "Oh, mercy on us, look at all the mud they're bringing with them and those blessed water weeds again. These beasts are a positive menace! You'll have to keep them on the recreation ground until the judges have been round again." He clapped his hands loudly at Sauro as the animal turned his head towards the rose garden. Jed was really thankful to get the animals back home.

Jed and his friends spent every spare minute with the dinosaurs. Then school broke up. And how better to spend one's summer holidays than looking after two placid prehistoric monsters?

As Jed had foreseen, Sauro followed Dino down to the river every morning and cooled his bulky body in the water. One morning when Jed returned from the river with Dino and Sauro he was delighted to find several bales of straw propped against the village hall.

He called out to his father, busy with a roller, "I'll get them bedded down really comfortably."

'That's right, Jed," replied Mr Watkins, pausing from his labours for a moment. "Make sure they've got enough food and water, and always see they're as clean as possible."

There wasn't nearly enough straw for such large creatures, but Jed and his friends did the best they could, spreading a quantity on the ground before Dino and Sauro squatted down. Jed ran off and returned with a pitchfork, with which he carefully frisked up the straw all round the dinosaurs. "They look just like two swans on a nest," he chuckled.

"Fat swans!" laughed Mr Watkins, coming to take a closer look.

The Parish Clerk came down the lane, calling out as

he drew near Jed. "I thought it was a good idea to have the straw delivered and I hope these beasts will be content to stay here quietly today. I have a feeling the judges are coming this afternoon. The streets have been swept clean and my garden looks much tidier with the new roses. I'll brook no nonsense from Dino and Sauro this time, *so keep them away from the village this afternoon!*"

"Oh, you can safely leave Dino and Sauro to me, sir," replied Jed confidently. "I'll keep them here all afternoon." When he was alone with the animals, Jed wagged his finger at them. "Now, you heard what the Parish Clerk said, so don't dare move," he told them. "I'll be keeping an eye on you both." He ran home. Several times during the midday meal he got up and went to the back door of the cottage, from where he could see the dinosaurs.

"For goodness' sake, Jed, don't leave the table again until you've finished your meal. Take my word for it, those two great lumps of mischief are far too comfortable to move off again just yet," said his mother.

"They only think of eating, drinking and sleeping," put in his father. "What a life! Wish I had a job like that."

After the meal, Jed helped his mother. "Can I go now, please?" he asked, when the last dish had been dried and put away.

"Oh, all right," she replied. "Off you go. I can't think what you found to do before those two creatures came into our lives."

Jed ran out – and stopped short in horror.

"They've disappeared!" he yelled.

Mr Watkins, who was having a much-needed nap, was very annoyed. "What's that? Gone, you say? Good heavens, Jed go and find them before the Parish Clerk sets eyes on them!"

Jed's short legs covered the ground at record speed. He followed a trail of straw. There were strands blowing gaily about in the breeze before festooning the trees, and strands trodden down into the gutters by giant feet. As Jed rounded the corner into the street, Dino's tail was disappearing over the river bridge, but Sauro had stopped outside the Parish Clerk's house and was making a meal of the new roses.

Jed hung back guiltily when he saw the Parish Clerk's plump figure, spectacles pushed back on to his forehead and newspaper in hand, appear at the front door. The Clerk let out a roar that brought Mr Holloway rushing out of his house on the opposite side of the street.

"Great Scott, Mr Parish Clerk, you did give me a fright. Whatever's the matter?" asked the headmaster.

"Matter? Matter? Can't you see – my roses – all this straw!" His voice rose to a shriek. "Those two horrible hefty monsters are at it again!"

Sauro was enjoying the roses. Had his brain been larger than a hen's egg, it might have occurred to him how kind it was of the Parish Clerk to keep providing him with such delicacies.

As it was, the Clerk was nearly beside himself, and

when he looked up the street and saw Jed cowering in a gateway and, beyond him, two men appearing round the corner, his rage knew no bounds. He jumped up and down, threw the newspaper on the pavement and stamped on it. "Here come the judges," he hissed. "This is more than I can bear." He turned to Sauro. "Be off, you great thieving monstrosity!"

Sauro decided to leave a few roses for the next visit and his bulky figure shuffled off down the road after Dino. The Parish Clerk, breathing heavily, watched him go.

"We'd be much better off with ten elephants," he sighed. "They wouldn't take up any more room. As it is, we might just as well own two useless mountains with a long tail and neck attached to each."

The two judges came up to him. "Fine beasts, those two dinosaurs of yours," one said admiringly, watching Sauro's tail disappearing from view. "Never seen anything like them before."

"Nothing in the whole wide world resembles them, believe me," said the Clerk.

The judges strolled up one side of the street, looking all around them, and came back down the other side. They opened out their marking sheets and consulted together.

"Street tidiness?" and shook their heads.

"Absence of litter?" They pursed up their lips and frowned.

"Tidiness of gardens?" They cast their eyes at the

Parish Clerk's garden. "Not a very good year for your roses, is it?" commented one.

"Well, we'll just take a look at the recreation ground," he continued. "Perhaps we'll find an improvement there," and off they went, tut-tutting to themselves.

The Parish Clerk, straws sticking out of his hair, heaved a great sigh. "Ah, well, that's the end of that. We'll be scratched from the 'possibles' list. There'll be no cup for us." He looked at Jed and then stared hard at the headmaster. "And if anyone dares to tell me again that those two gigantic, lazy, over-fed useless fiends are going to *earn their keep*, I'll . . . I'll . . . I don't know what I'll do! You ought to be helping me get rid of them, instead of always saying how valuable they are to us."

CHAPTER 3

Dino and Sauro in the film

Just as the Parish Clerk turned to go back into the house, a large, chauffeur-driven car drew up. The door was opened and out stepped a tall, smartly-dressed man. Jed crept forward shyly. He recognized the film director who had wanted to buy Dino.

The Parish Clerk looked back. "Good afternoon," he said sourly. "Fancy anyone visiting a 'Bottom of the list for the Best-Kept Village competition' village – and all due to those two dinosaurs. I wish with all my heart I'd sold Dino to you. I expect you've heard we've got another one now?"

The visitor didn't answer immediately. He looked

eagerly up and down the street. At length he said, "I've got a proposal to put to you which will bring in a nice sum of money."

"Anything to do with dinosaurs?" asked Mr Holloway, grinning. "They're not very popular around here at present."

The director laughed. "Well, in a way," he replied.

"Good old Dino," exclaimed Mr Holloway.

"Good old Sauro," echoed Jed cheerfully.

But the Parish Clerk was still truculent. "I don't believe those two great barrels of destruction could be of help to anyone," he scowled.

"It's like this," explained the director. "My company is making a film about medieval times. Now, the mud and straw have given this street an old-fashioned look – just right for one of the scenes in the film." Stepping into the middle of the road, he gazed up at the roofs of the houses and shops.

The Parish Clerk's face had brightened, but now he said gloomily, "I know what you're thinking. There weren't any television aerials in those days."

"True, true, but what's to stop us dismantling them for one day?"

"People would never agree," gasped the Clerk. "They wouldn't be able to look in at their favourite programmes."

"Phooh! We'd get a move on with the filming and they'd only miss one day's entertainment. *And* we'll pay five pounds to each resident as compensation for the loss of viewing."

So the Clerk and the director interviewed all the householders, who readily agreed to the suggestion. (Especially when they heard about the five pounds!)

"That's very satisfactory," said the director. "If it suits you, I'll be back in a week's time to start filming and I'll keep in touch with you in the meantime." Taking one last look up at the village street, he said, "Good afternoon," to everyone, waved his hat at Jed, got into the car and was driven off.

Everyone gathered round for a conference. The headmaster turned to the Parish Clerk. "How's that for the dinosaurs 'earning their keep'? There's no money in a Best-Kept Village competition cup. This is much better."

"Of course it is," agreed the Clerk. "Haven't I always said the dinosaurs are a credit to the village? We're indeed very, very lucky to own two such fabulous beasts and don't let us forget it."

Jed glanced at Mr Holloway.

"But there's one very important matter to be decided," continued the Parish Clerk. "How on earth are we going to prevent the dinosaurs charging up and down the street while the filming is taking place?"

"Oh, really, Mr Parish Clerk, do be accurate!" remonstrated Mr Holloway. "The dinosaurs are quite incapable of lifting all four feet of the ground at one time let alone charging up and down."

"Well, anyhow, they've got to be kept away from the street. Now, Jed, what are *you* going to do about it? No one else has much control over those two beauties. Are you prepared to stay with them all day and miss the fun?"

"Oh, yes, sir, I don't mind missing the filming. I'd much rather stay with Dino and Sauro. I'll get them down to the river and back again at crack of dawn. Then they'll be content to stay on the recreation ground for the rest of the day. They'll be very well behaved, I promise, sir."

"All right, then, that's settled. Whatever happens, *keep them out of the village on that day!*"

A week later, Jed got up very early and fed the dinosaurs. Then he led them through the village and down to the river. He watched as they waded in until only a few feet of dinosaur necks were exposed.

When Jed thought they had been in long enough, he gave the signal for them to come out. He waited . . . and waited . . . and waited. Nothing happened. Time was getting on. Poor Jed! He whistled until he was blue in the face. Then he took off his shoes and socks and waded into the river as far as he dared, calling to the two animals.

Eventually, Dino decided to move and rose very slowly out of the water and came towards the bank. Sauro followed. It was a frustrating journey back for Jed. He had to hang about while the dinosaurs ate the leaves off the topmost branches of a tall tree, and again when they stopped to gaze – at nothing at all!

The Parish Clerk was already out and about. He would be, thought Jed. "Hurry up, for heaven's sake,

Jed," he said fussily. "It's getting late." As though it was all Jed's fault.

Mr Holloway came out of his house. "Good show, Jed," he said approvingly. "Just in time."

As Dino and Sauro made their way home, the first motor in the convoy of vehicles belonging to the film company drove into the village. Jed heaved a sigh of relief.

"Now Dino, and you too, Sauro, just settle down for the whole day," he encouraged in a loud voice, his head flung back so that he could peer up at them. As a special treat – or was it a bribe? – he fed them some bread soaked in milk, although he well knew that was now forbidden. And the animals settled down to chew.

Jed wasn't bothered about missing the filming. Dino and Sauro had taken to him more than to anyone else. Oh, yes, indeed, he would miss *anything* to be with them. He wasn't going to leave them this time. Oh, no! His mother had provided him with sandwiches and a bottle of orange squash. And at intervals a friend ran down the lane from the village and described what was going on.

"The rooftops look very strange without the aerials and the road is covered with wet straw and muddy pools – just like old streets we've seen on films!"

Later on the news was, "The cameras have been set up on gantries and the actors and actresses have changed into medieval costumes. It's wonderful! There's been nothing so exciting in the village since Dino came along."

The day wore on and Jed had no more news, because no one came to visit him. He could hear shouting and, occasionally, the clip-clop of horses' hooves. He started to fidget. Dino and Sauro appeared to be fast asleep. They'd curled themselves up with heads on long necks tucked in towards their bodies. They didn't stop munching, however, and bits of leaves stuck out from the corners of their mouths alongside their whiskers.

Jed leaned over and rubbed his hands over Dino's neck, talking to him soothingly. "I *told* the Parish Clerk you'd be as good as gold. Can't think why he gets so angry. This village would still be going on in the same sleepy old way if you hadn't been discovered."

Jed ate the last sandwich and noisily sucked the remains of the orange squash through straws. Then, chewing a piece of grass, he got up and strolled about, kicking at a loose, grassy sod. He walked right round the two massive beasts, deciding that it was a distance of a quarter of a mile, or – at least – one eighth of a mile. And when he stood between Dino and the wall of the hall, it was as dark as being in a tunnel.

His footsteps took him a little bit farther away, in the direction of the village, as a matter of fact, and a little farther still. Not for one minute did he intend leaving them. Oh, no! As he rounded the corner he glanced back. Dino and Sauro were sound asleep.

Jed hardly recognized the village. Men, women and children in period costume were standing about on the pavements and a man dressed in a smock was waiting to push up the street a rickety old hand-cart piled high with vegetables. Old-fashioned baskets, as well as iron pots and pans, hung from hooks outside some of the shops.

The "stars" stood ready in the doorway of the inn, and the director, seated on a tall stool near to the cameras, yelled through a microphone, "That's perfect. Get ready for the final take."

Jed was thrilled with it all. But, suddenly, he felt the earth tremble. He'd had that sensation before. Broad, padded feet were plodding towards him. They'd moved! At first, he was proud because they had followed him, but then, when he thought of the damage they might do, he was horrified.

Cupping his mouth in his hands, he shouted at the top of his lungs. "Wait a minute, sir, please don't shoot yet. Dino and Sauro are coming! I'll drive them back."

But once on the move Dino and Sauro came on like a couple of slow-moving bulldozers. Jed was forced to walk backwards in front of them, and the Parish Clerk, hair fringing his bald head standing on end, kept step with Jed and tried to halt Dino, who was in the lead as usual. The villagers were enjoying themselves and cheered from their vantage point on a raised terrace, out of the range of the cameras.

Losing his balance, the Parish Clerk fell over backwards and rolled into the gutter out of the way of the dinosaurs' feet. The stars ran hurriedly into the inn, while the extras slipped and fell about in the roadway.

The handcart was knocked over and all the vegetables rolled about in the road.

"Take!" ordered the director, breathlessly. The cameramen, eyes bulging, took no notice of him. "Take! Take!" roared the director again, standing on his stool in order to get a better view and shaking – as Jed thought – with rage. So the cameramen filmed the scene of pandemonium and turned their cameras hastily on the dinosaurs as they drew level.

As can be imagined the Parish Clerk, helped to his feet by Mr Holloway, was in despair. "I knew this would happen. I just *knew* it!" he cried. "Trust those two to spoil everything. 'Earn their keep' did you say?" he asked Mr Holloway. "'Well behaved' did you promise?" he sneered at Jed. "We'll be charged for spoiling the film instead of being paid for cooperating. *And* we'll have to pay for the vegetables – look at those two hulking brutes now!"

Dino had discovered the vegetables rolling about in the roadway. He helped himself to a few and then, as there wasn't room for two dinosaurs abreast, moved on ahead to allow Sauro to have his share. Jed was crestfallen. Everything had been ruined and it was all his fault. He turned hesitantly to the Parish Clerk. "I'm very sorry, sir," he said. "I'm to blame. I shouldn't have left them, not even for a single minute." He couldn't resist adding, "They followed me."

The Parish Clerk rolled his eyes skywards. "Ah, well," he moaned. "It's only to be expected of those two prodigies of ours, I suppose. But I'll never get used to them, *never, never, never,*" and he stamped his foot three times in emphasis.

The director came running up. To Jed's surprise, he was shaking with mirth. "What's the matter with you all?" he cried. "Everything's fine, just fine. That film will make a gorgeous comedy 'short'. Haven't seen anything so funny for years. People slipping all over the place, vegetables rolling into the gutter. And those two gargantuan beasts! Cheer up, do, Mr Parish Clerk. I'm prepared to pay you an extra fifty pounds for that film. It won't take us very long to get the street prepared again for the proper filming. No real harm has been done."

Mr Holloway smiled at Jed as the director continued. "Now, then, Jed, do you think you can get Dino and Sauro down to the river – they're headed that way – and keep them there for a while?"

"Oh, yes, sir, I'll see to them," sang out Jed, already on his way. "Come on, Dino! Hurry up, Sauro!" he shouted. After a lengthy pause, Dino sauntered after Jed. Sauro raised his head, a large cabbage dangling from his mouth,and decided to follow.

Glancing back, Jed noticed a broad grin on the Parish Clerk's face! Perhaps, one day, the Clerk would *really* appreciate Dino and Sauro.

Jed put on his "thinking cap". Now, what could the dinosaurs do to make the Parish Clerk really grateful? Something *very* helpful?

CHAPTER 4

Dino and Sauro at the fête

Next day, Jed was still thinking how Dino and Sauro could really impress the Parish Clerk. Now, what was worrying the Clerk more than anything? He'd got it – money! That was it. Dino and Sauro could help to raise funds at the annual fête next week, couldn't they? Next time Jed met the Parish Clerk, who was talking to Mr Holloway in the street, he told him about his idea.

"Get people to pay *five pence* each to view those two bloated beasts? You must be mad, Jed. In any case, don't forget they'll tower over everyone and everything on the ground. No one will want to *pay* to see them."

Jed felt hurt. Fancy anyone saying things like that about the dinosaurs."Yes, I know everyone will be able to see them, sir," he replied. 'But visitors might care to have a close look at them. I thought of roping them round and letting in a few people at a time."

Mr Holloway was more encouraging. "A trench would be the only sure method of keeping the dinosaurs captive," he said. "But, on second thoughts, it would have to be such a whacking big trench, it would take a gang of workmen about a week to dig one!"

"Those animals take up far too much room as it is," said the Clerk.

"But it's not a bad idea of Jed's to rope them in," continued Mr Holloway. "We need a really good profit at this year's fête. As you know, the community hall is costing far more than the budget."

"You never spoke a truer word!" answered the Clerk.

"And it would be disastrous if it should rain," continued the headmaster. "You wouldn't take my advice and insure against a wet day."

'Stuff and nonsense! It's never yet rained on fête day. I'm not going to be bitten like that – paying out good money for insurance when it isn't necessary. I wasn't born yesterday," cried the Clerk.

He turned to Jed. "All right, then, young fellow-me-lad, do what you like with those two darlings of yours, but two pence a time is quite enough for anyone to pay."

"Should be two pounds a time," muttered Jed, under his breath.

The sky was cloudless on the morning of the fête. After the dinosaurs had had their early morning bathe, and had settled down by the hall, Jed and his friends got busy. Plenty of straw was laid down, green vegetables were to hand and the trough was filled with water. Jed's father had provided several coils of rope, with which the boys fenced in the two stupendous exhibits.

Hands behind his back, the Parish Clerk strolled round the ground, supervising everyone. Last-minute checks were being made on the model railway and the fun fair was ready to go. The Parish Clerk stopped near the dinosaurs. A large notice met his gaze:

FIVE PENCE TO COME CLOSER TO
THE GREATEST BEASTS ON EARTH,

it read.

"It should read,

TWO PENCE TO VIEW THE
GREATEST NUISANCES ON EARTH,"

exploded the Clerk, turning to a rebellious Jed.

At two o'clock, many anxious glances were cast up at the darkening sky. "Only a passing cloud," said the Parish Clerk reassuringly.

"I sincerely hope so," replied Mr Holloway. "But

it's a very, very big cloud and it's taking a long time to pass over."

As soon as the ceremony of "opening the fête" had been performed, Jed and his friends started doing a roaring trade. There was already a queue waiting to get nearer to the greatest beasts on earth. Jed took the five pence pieces eagerly. He had always loved fête day – the smell of candy floss and hot dogs, the music and the milling crowds.

Dino seemed to revel in all the attention, but Sauro was restless. Ears pricked, he turned his head this way and that, towards the music coming from the bandstand and the blare from the fun fair. He seemed to be on the alert all the time for the first sign of danger.

The "queen" was due to be crowned at three o'clock and the film director, floral crown in hand, stood beside her on a small wooden stage especially erected for the occasion. The Parish Clerk, looking very important and grand, was also on the stage with the committee.

Unfortunately, just at this moment, Sauro decided he had had enough. Before Jed realized what he was up to, he had moved off, breaking the ropes and pulling the posts out of the ground as he went. He glanced uneasily at the roundabouts and clicked his tail contemptuously towards the model railway. People fled in all directions as he made for the stage. The Parish Clerk jumped down hastily and ran forward.

"Oh, no! Oh, no!" he screamed. "Jed, where are

you? Head him off! We're just going to crown the queen."

"I'm here, sir," panted Jed, running right underneath Sauro's stomach. Sauro was now near enough to the stage to stretch out his neck and go after what had attracted him – brightly coloured, delicious-looking flowers, including roses! Before the director realized what was happening, Sauro had nibbled at the edge of the floral crown. Snatching it away quickly, the director put it behind his back. But he was no match for Sauro, who butted him in the ribs.

The director gave up. Laughing heartily, he placed the crown on the top of Sauro's outstretched head. "I hereby crown you 'Queen of the Fête'," he shouted through a microphone.

The Parish Clerk was simply appalled. Never before had anything so disgraceful happened to him. He would never live this down. The shame of it – and the real uncrowned queen running crying off the stage!

Sauro seemed very annoyed. He tried, without success, to shake the crown off his head. But, no matter, he had noticed more flowers. The fact that they were on the head of a plump committee lady didn't matter. He bent his long neck and daintily took the hat from the head of the astonished lady. Turning, he trundled off in the direction of the village, one floral hat dangling from his mouth and the crown perched on top of his head. Dino decided to follow him.

"Wait until I get my hands on you, you thieving, ugly ruffian! I'll show you . . . I'll give you what for . . . I'll . . . ' The Parish Clerk's agonized voice fairly rent the air.

Jed hurried off and wandered unhappily round the fair ground. Such a pity. He could have taken a lot of money and the Parish Clerk would have been so pleased. Ah, well, perhaps he'd be able to think of something else. But he'd have to allow the Clerk time to get over this unseemly episode.

To add to Jed's misery, the rain started to fall and it wasn't long before it became a deluge. The band struggled on dismally, but were eventually forced to cover their instruments and run for shelter. A few youngsters were determined to spend their pocket-money, so the fun fair carried on for a time, but they too had to give up. It was a sorry end to fête day.

With hair plastered over his forehead and rain trickling down his neck, Jed stood forlornly outside the officials' tent. His father looked out and saw him. "Come in here out of the rain, Jed," he called.

"Pity you didn't take out that insurance," the headmaster was saying mildly to the Parish Clerk as Jed crept into the tent. "We would at least have had that much compensation money."

"Never mind about the insurance. What about those dratted dinosaurs making such a mockery of the whole thing?" cried the Clerk. "Whoever heard of a dinosaur being crowned queen! We'll be the laughing stock of the whole country. That reporter of ours will have sent the news to the national press, trust her."

He paused, glaring balefully at two policemen, who

had appeared at the tent opening. "Oh, come in, do," he shouted. "More trouble? Well, I'm resigned to anything these days."

"Anyone round here own two dinosaurs?" asked the sergeant, keeping a straight face.

"Not them again! Oh, no! Break the news gently, please, I feel weak." The Parish Clerk sat down heavily on a canvas chair, which promptly sank into the mud and deposited him on the ground. Jed rushed to help him on to his feet again.

"Come on, tell me the worst," spluttered the Clerk. "I suppose I'll have to take the blame the same as usual. Why ever did I agree to keep them? They'll have to . . ."

"Oh, no, indeed, they won't have to go," put in Mr Holloway quickly.

"Well, what have they been up to? Let's hear it," ordered the Clerk.

"It's like this," began the sergeant. "This afternoon, just as two gentlemen – in a hurry, they were – emerged from a certain building in the main street of the village, Sauro comes strolling along. He had something on his head. I don't know what it was."

"It was a crown," muttered the Clerk.

"A what?"

"Oh, never mind, do go on."

"Well, the din of aircraft passing overhead startled Sauro, who lurched to one side, pinning the two men against the wall as they rushed out of the building.

"They were terrified. We heard their shouts and

screams for help down at the police station," said the policeman, shaking his head. "It was pitiful."

"Oh, dear me, how shameful," said the Clerk, a hand to his lips to stop them trembling.

"That's not all!"

"I don't think I can bear any more today," murmured the Clerk.

But the sergeant went on relentlessly. "A few yards farther up the road a high-powered car was parked alongside the pavement."

"Well, what happened to that?" asked the Clerk fearfully.

"Dino comes along. He prods Sauro, who moves forward, leaving the two men prostrate on the pavement. Another jet streaks across the sky. Sauro bumps into the car, crashing it against a wall, trapping the driver inside the car."

"And I've never heard anything like *his* shrieks. Terrible!" added the policeman.

"I don't want to hear any more," pleaded the Parish Clerk. "We'll be sued for heavy damages, I know. Let's hope we can afford to pay them." He turned to the headmaster. "'Earn their keep' did you say?"

Mr Holloway was stroking his chin thoughtfully, in the way Jed knew meant something had occurred to him. "*Which* building did you say the men were leaving?" he asked.

"I didn't say, sir," replied the sergeant, grinning from ear to ear. "I was waiting for someone to ask me that. It was the bank."

"But it's Saturday," replied Mr Holloway. "The bank closes at 11 o'clock."

"Exactly, sir. These men were unwanted clients, bank robbers, in fact. Thinking everything would be quiet in the village, most people being at the fête, they gained entrance to the bank through a back door. They overwhelmed the bank manager and clerks, who were working late. Then they collected all the money and made their way out through the front door, where the car was waiting for them."

He heaved a sigh of great satisfaction. "I can't tell you how proud our small police force is to have had a hand in capturing three cunning and dangerous criminals."

"And all because of Dino and Sauro!" burst out Jed, unable to keep quiet any longer.

"All because of these two lovelies," agreed the sergeant. "Full credit must be given to them for capturing the thieves."

"A good day's work," commented Mr Holloway. "I'm only sorry it turned out such a wet day for the fête."

"Oh, bother the rain," shouted the Parish Clerk exuberantly. "Let's go and see if those animals are all right. What a boon it is to own two such intelligent beasts."

"Come on, Jed," said Mr Holloway, patting the boy on the shoulder. "You're certainly bringing up your two charges to be very helpful."

"They're always willing, sir," answered Jed, with

satisfaction. "They're the cleverest animals, as well as the largest, in the world."

"I agree to the latter statement, Jed," smiled Mr Holloway. "But as to being the cleverest, well, I have my doubts – but they'll do!"

CHAPTER 5

The Professor arrives

One day, after school, Jed was looking after Dino and Sauro, spraying them with a hosepipe and rubbing parts of them within his reach with a hard-bristled brush. Looking up from his task, Jed saw the Parish Clerk, letter in hand, approaching across the recreation ground.

The Clerk had been very pleased with the dinosaurs lately. In fact, he was more enthusiastic about them than anyone else in the village. "How fortunate we are to own two such magnificent beasts. I wouldn't be without them for anything," he would say. Jed hoped everything was still all right.

The Parish Clerk waved the letter in the air. "I've got something here that will interest you, Jed," he called out. He gazed at the dinosaurs. "I'm glad you're taking such an interest in their appearance. They're growing into fine-looking animals." Glancing down the lane, he continued, "Ah, good. Here comes your headmaster. I'd like him to hear me read this letter."

Mr Holloway came up to them. "My word, Jed," he said "The dinosaurs are in fine fettle. Sauro's hide has lost its dingy look. And as for Dino – well, he positively glows with health."

"There isn't a finer beast in the whole world, sir," said Jed. "Or a better-natured one."

"Or a faster-moving one – I don't think!" The Clerk laughed boisterously. "But, seriously, I agree with you, they're in excellent condition and you wouldn't find better-behaved animals anywhere."

Mr Holloway raised his eyebrows and Jed hastily agreed. "You wouldn't, sir, oh, indeed, you wouldn't."

"Which brings me to this letter," continued the Parish Clerk. "I was just going to tell Jed, Mr Holloway, that I've received a communication from a Professor Klott, who lives in a town in eastern Europe – one with an outlandish name. What *do* you think the silly ass says?"

Mr Holloway and Jed shook their heads.

"I'll read it to you – the silly idiot! – just listen to this: 'News has reached me that you are the owner of two so-called dinosaurs, the same having been dug up alive out of a chalk-pit. I feel it my bounden duty to inform you that, in my opinion, the animals are *not* dinosaurs, there having been no such creatures on this planet for over 200 million years. In my opinion, they are giant lizards of a type common in New Guinea. As I shall be in England next month, I hope you will permit me to visit your village and prove my theory' ,"

"Giant lizards – look at them!" scoffed Mr Holloway. "They're dinosaurs every inch – every yard, I should say – of them."

"Lizards. Best joke this millennium," roared the Clerk cheerfully.

"Well, they belong to the same family as lizards, but that isn't what the Professor means," said Mr Holloway.

"Let him come," cried the Clerk contemptuously. "We'll give him the shock of his life."

"He'll certainly be surprised," commented the headmaster, smiling at the two animals, whose heads were towering over the roof of the community hall.

"The dinosaurs have been doing splendidly lately, one way and another, but we could do with more publicity, especially abroad, and this may be the means of getting it," said the Parish Clerk.

"Keep up the good work of grooming them, Jed," advised Mr Holloway.

Jed needed no urging although it was hard work. His father helped him to make a trench for the water to drain into after the animals had been hosed down daily. "They like lots of cool water in summer, as they can't stand extremes of heat or cold," Mr Watkins explained.

The Parish Clerk and Mr Holloway often came along to keep an eye on the dinosaurs. "We may be able to make capital out of this business with the Professor, and then we can begin to think seriously about shelter for them before the winter," announced the Clerk.

"That's a 'must', I'm afraid," replied Mr Holloway. "I doubt very much whether they would be able to stand a severe winter without some kind of protection."

"Hm," said the Clerk. "Well, if they earn enough they'll merit a shelter." He smiled at Dino and Sauro.

Jed spent all his spare time caring for the animals. "We hardly ever see you these days, Jed, except when you come home for meals and sleep," complained his mother.

"Oh, but Dino and Sauro must be in really first-class condition when the Professor arrives," replied Jed proudly.

Early one Friday morning, the Parish Clerk came running down the lane. "The Professor will be here tomorrow, Jed," he cried. Jed looked up from his task of preparing the dinosaurs' breakfast. The Clerk went on, "He hasn't given us much notice, has he? But, never mind, he couldn't see two finer-looking, better-cared-for animals anywhere, thanks to you, Jed. Tell your father, will you, before you go to school, and I'll go along and give Mr Holloway the news."

That evening, Jed and his father gave the animals a thorough grooming. Jed was so excited he could hardly sleep that night. In the morning, when he went out, there was no sign of the dinosaurs. They'll make their own way back from the river, he thought.

But when he met the Parish Clerk and Mr Holloway in the village, the Clerk said, "I think it would be advisable if you got them back to the recreation ground straight away, Jed. It's going to be very hot today and they might take it into their heads to stay in the river."

"It would be funny if we had to say to the Professor: 'There they are, four eyes, four ears and two noses,'" laughed Mr Holloway.

"I'll go and fetch them," said Jed, running off towards the river.

He looked upstream, he looked downstream, but he couldn't see any sign of the dinosaurs. He waited in case they had submerged completely for a brief spell. But no, there wasn't a ripple and the fallen leaves lay motionless on the glassy surface of the water.

Jed was very worried. Perhaps they were in the thicket alongside the railway line? He ran off to continue the search, but there was no trace of the dinosaurs anywhere. Reluctantly, Jed rushed back to the village and arrived breathless at the Parish Clerk's house.

"I can't find them *anywhere*," he cried, very near to tears.

"Can't find them? Oh, no! Oh, no! They can't have disappeared again!" He flayed his arms about like a windmill. "Get a move on, Jed. Do something. Find that couple of troublemakers at any cost."

Poor Jed ran home. He told his father and mother what had happened. "No peace, now," sighed his mother. But his father said, "Now, don't worry, Jed. They've been missing before and we've always found them."

"Yes, I know, but there isn't much time. The Professor is due here in an hour or so."

All the boys in the village turned out to help in the search. They spent all morning looking here, there and everywhere, until they were tired out. Jed felt his legs wouldn't support him much longer.

When they finally arrived back in the village, there was a small group in the street. The Parish Clerk and Mr Holloway were talking to a tall, thin, supercilious-looking man wearing a light mackintosh and a trilby hat with a feather stuck in the side. The Professor, thought Jed!

The Parish Clerk was very, very angry. "Don't believe me, you say? But everyone here can vouch for Dino and Sauro." He spread out his arms to include the curious villagers crowding round. "That's all very well," snorted the Professor. "But where are these animals? Don't tell me creatures of the size you claim they are could vanish into thin air. If their necks are so long, how could they hide? Are they afraid of me, me, the mighty Professor Klott, world-authority on all kinds of reptiles? Tell me that, are they?"

Almost nose to nose, the Parish Clerk and the

Professor glared at one another. The Professor hadn't finished. "Now I had expected that at least there would have been a band playing to welcome me – and a procession led by the so-called dinosaurs!"

Jed saw the Parish Clerk clench his fists and hold his arms rigid at his sides. The Professor was going too far with his taunts.

But Mr Holloway was stroking his chin. "Procession, did you say?" he murmured. "Procession?" he repeated loudly. "That's it! Come on, Mr Parish Clerk, and you too, Professor. And you, of course, Jed. Jump into my car and I'll take you to see the two greatest phenomena on earth."

"I hope you're serious, Mr Holloway," cried the Parish Clerk, still shaking with rage and mortification. He climbed into the back of the open car with the Professor, and Jed leapt into the passenger seat beside the driver.

Mr Holloway drove towards the nearby town. Jed was hopeful, but mystified. There was no circus in the town to steal the dinosaurs. What had Mr Holloway in mind?

As they entered the main street of the town, they could hear music, and crowds of excited children and grown-ups lined the pavements. A policeman came forward and held up the traffic.

"Hear anything, Professor? The band's approaching and the procession won't be long in following," smiled Mr Holloway.

"It's University Rag Day!" shouted Jed suddenly.

"The students must have kidnapped Dino and Sauro in the night."

"Here they come, Professor! Here they come!" The Parish Clerk stood on the seat of the car and threw his hat up into the air. It fell down into the crowd and was lost for ever.

First came red-coated bandsmen, led by a drummer, playing stirring music. They were followed by several colourful "floats". Students in all kinds of costumes ran about rattling tin collecting boxes under people's noses. The Parish Clerk waved them away. "No, no, no. You ought to be paying *me*," he cried.

Then came the dinosaurs. "Dino! Sauro!" shouted Jed at the top of his voice. "I'm here. I'm here." The Professor's eyes fairly boggled. He hissed through his teeth in amazement. The Parish Clerk dug him hard in the ribs. "Is that a dinosaur, or isn't it?" he asked. The Professor moistened his dry lips and nodded and nodded and nodded.

Suddenly, everything was forced to halt. Dino had recognized Jed. His long, long neck came down towards the car. The Professor, and the Clerk – who had never quite got used to the dinosaurs – scrambled out in a most undignified manner. Everything was in a state of confusion. As usual, however, Mr Holloway took command.

"I'm afraid you'll have to lead them back home, Jed. We'll follow in the car," he said.

The crowd cheered and roared as the massive beasts passed down the street. The powerful tails thrashed about a little but Jed knew that Dino and Sauro had lost their fear of humans and wouldn't lash out dangerously. The Professor, back in the car, was overwhelmed. "I'd never, never, never have believed it if I hadn't seen them with my very own eyes," he kept saying over and over again. "What a tale I shall have to tell when I get back home."

"Well, I told you all along they are dinosaurs," said the Parish Clerk complacently.

The Professor departed that evening full of apologies for not believing that Dino and Sauro were really dinosaurs, and he promised to make amends by spreading the news all round the world.

Next day, the Parish Clerk, Mr Holloway and Jed were on the recreation ground, discussing the previous day's events, when two shamefaced students arrived. They said they were very sorry they had kidnapped Dino and Sauro. "But we thought they would be such an attraction and bring in a lot of money for charity," one student said, in justification.

"That's all very well," fussed the Parish Clerk. "But what about the money it costs us to feed, to say nothing of trying to house them?"

"Well, we've heard about the dinosaurs needing a shelter for the winter," the student continued. "So we've all clubbed together – there are a lot us – and we've bought a disused hangar for them, which we hope you'll accept."

"A hangar?" cried the Parish Clerk, aghast.

"A hangar?" laughed Jed. "Just the very thing.

They'll both be able to get in comfortably and snuggle down in the winter."

"A hangar? That's a good idea," smiled Mr Holloway. "I'm beginning to think you're right, Jed. The dinosaurs are clever – in their own way. At least, they've earned themselves a cosy home for the winter."

"They're not doing too badly," agreed the Parish Clerk. "But I can't imagine what an ugly contraption like a hangar is going to look like alongside our brand new community hall."

He *would* have to say something like that, thought Jed disgustedly.

CHAPTER 6

Dino wins the race

Jed wished the Parish Clerk wouldn't go on so about the hangar spoiling the look of the new hall. What did that matter so long as Dino and Sauro were comfortable? Trust the Parish Clerk to make a fuss about nothing.

Mr Holloway had a suggestion. "Why not site the hangar on the out-of-use allotments? The ground might as well be used for something."

The Parish Clerk gave the matter some thought. Then, "Not a bad idea," he cried. "Not a bad idea at all. I'll discuss it with my council at the next meeting." The council voted in favour of the proposal and, in due course, the dinosaurs' new home was erected on the old allotments, a little way down the lane from the village hall.

All the villagers and several students from the university turned out for the opening ceremony. It was a very gay occasion. Everybody cheered as the Parish Clerk opened the doors of the hangar and, led by Jed, the dinosaurs strolled into their new quarters, snuffling all round before finally settling down. The hangar was very roomy and high enough for them to get in easily, so long as they lowered their heads, which they quickly learned to do.

The Parish Clerk announced that he was very pleased with the new accommodation. As though *he'd* provided it, instead of having grumbled about it, thought Jed indignantly.

"Now, when we want to keep the dinosaurs out of the way, Jed, it'll be simple," boomed the Parish Clerk. "Just settle them inside the hangar and close the doors."

Keep them hidden away! Fancy *anyone* not wanting to see Dino and Sauro. Jed couldn't believe the Parish Clerk was serious.

"Next week is a case in point," continued the Clerk. "As you know, royalty will be passing through this village on their way to the races. At all costs, the roads must be kept clear of ordinary traffic then. That means those two mischief-makers will have to be kept in their quarters. Too risky even to allow them down to the river. They'd only do something daft."

"But won't they want to see Dino and Sauro?" asked Jed, astonished.

"No, no. They're only passing through the village. Mind you, if we're lucky they might, at some future date, make a special visit to view the dinosaurs. That would be something. My word, we'd be famous all right then."

On the day of the races – a school holiday – the village was bedecked with flags and bunting and looked very gay in the sunshine. Police were on duty controlling the traffic. Everybody turned out. The village was spick and span and the Parish Clerk was very pleased with it all. Only one thought saddened him. "What a pity it isn't judging day for Best-Kept Village competition," he sighed.

"Some people are never satisfied," retorted the headmaster.

"Dino and Sauro tucked away comfortably, Jed?" called out the Clerk jovially.

He didn't wait for an answer, which was just as well. Dino and Sauro were *not* in the hangar. In fact, Jed hadn't the least idea where they were. He'd been down to the river, but there was no trace of them there. But he wasn't bothered. He knew from past experience they'd turn up eventually. So long as they didn't put in an appearance before the royal cars had passed through the village!

Jed quailed at the thought of the huge bodies blocking the street, holding everything up. Sauro would probably go for the elegant hats on the ladies' heads. And how embarrassing that would be.

There was a stirring among the crowds lining the pavements and Jed put such awful thoughts from his mind. Soon, the first car, standard on the front gaily fluttering in the breeze, came into view, slowing down as it passed the cheering crowds. Jed waved his flag as energetically as the rest.

When the last car had disappeared round the corner, Jed and his friends began to look for Dino and Sauro. But there was no sign of them anywhere and Jed began to get really worried. It was nearly 12 o'clock and the search had to be abandoned.

After the midday meal, Jed said to his father, "I don't want to go to the fair this afternoon. I'd much rather stay and look for Dino and Sauro."

"Not go to the fair!" cried Mr Watkins. "Don't be silly, lad. The races are held only once a year and you always spend the afternoon at the fair with the other boys. So be off with you, the coach will be waiting. Keep a look-out as you drive along and I'll make inquiries round here. Somebody must have seen them."

The fair was one of the highlights of the year and Jed entered into the fun and spent his pocket-money as freely as the others, but he couldn't entirely forget that Dino and Sauro were missing again. Where could they be this time? The Parish Clerk would be furious if he found out. It was a good job he was at the races with Mr Holloway.

The afternoon wore on. All pocket-money had been spent and Jed and his friends drifted round the fair.

Jed was startled when, over the loud-speakers, came an announcement. "Jed Watkins, please. Is Jed Watkins on the fairground? He's wanted urgently at the race-course office at the main gate."

More trouble, thought Jed, running as fast as he could through the crowds. At the office, he found Mr Holloway and several officials waiting impatiently for him.

"Come on, Jed," urged Mr Holloway. "The race for the Gold Cup, the most important event, is due to start in a few minutes and – guess what? – Dino and Sauro are making their way on to the course. The Parish Clerk is nearly going mad, poor chap."

"Where have they been hiding?" Jed inquired, trying manfully to keep pace with the longer-legged grown-ups as they all made their way towards the race track.

"They've apparently been lurking behind trees to the north of the course. I imagine they must have been aware of the horse-boxes passing through the village last night. Some instinct probably led them to come over here to investigate. It's often impossible to understand animals' behaviour."

They sped along the outside rails bordering the race track. Some of the racegoers, pressed against the rails, were too engrossed watching the line-up of the horses to notice two large bodies looming up behind them. Others, however, glanced over their shoulders and saw the dinosaurs. They scattered hurriedly in all directions, their screams lost among the general hubbub.

The horses were eventually lined up and soon, after a lot of jostling, "They're off! They're off!" echoed round the course, as the favourite took the lead and raced away. The horses disappeared round the first bend as Jed and Mr Holloway rushed up to the dinosaurs. The Parish Clerk was running round the animals, imploring each in turn to halt.

Arms flapping wildly, the Clerk ran towards Jed. 'Oh, where on earth have you been, Jed?" he wailed. "Why didn't you come sooner? Stop them! Stop them!"

In spite of all Jed's efforts, however, Sauro crashed through the rail and he was on the race track. With a backward glance at Jed, Dino followed. People were amazed. Nothing like this had ever happened before. The two beasts, Dino on the stands side and Sauro over on the far side, made their dignified way along the track towards the finishing-post.

"Oh, oh, good heavens! The horses will be coming round the first lap in a minute," the Parish Clerk screamed. "They won't be able to get past. What shall we do? What *shall* we do? I've never been involved in anything so awful in all my life. This is the end. It's just too much. They'll have to . . . "

"Oh, that's quite enough. Don't let me hear you say *that* again, for goodness' sake," cried Mr Holloway impatiently.

"Get off the track, you clumsy great oafs," yelled the Parish Clerk. "Oh, oh, I knew it was too good to last. And all this talk of 'earning their keep'. I hope I'll never, never hear you speak those words again, Mr Holloway."

But Mr Holloway wasn't paying any attention to the distracted man. Horses, hooves pounding the turf, were rounding the bend. When they saw the dinosaurs ahead of them, the surprised jockeys leaned hard on their stirrups and pulled in the reins. Horses and riders – looking like pygmies behind two giants – fanned out all over the place.

The stands were in an uproar. Jed had a brief glimpse of some very important persons doubled up with laughter as, leading by a short head, Dino ambled in a leisurely manner past the winning-post. Such cheering and shouting had never before been heard on a racecourse. People came down from the stands and surged on to the track, surrounding Dino and Sauro, who had at last halted.

The officials turned to the unfortunate Parish Clerk. "I hope you realize this is a very serious matter, Mr Parish Clerk," one said. "Never, in the history of racing, have we experienced anything like this before."

"And never, in my career as Parish Clerk, has anything like this happened to me before," groaned the Clerk.

However, after a brief consultation, the officials decided to regard the first race as a false start. Jed succeeded in enticing Dino and Sauro off the track as the horses were lined up a second time. And – "They're off! They're off!" soon came from all sides again. The dinosaurs seemed to sense the growing excitement and weaved and stretched their long necks towards the royal box, as the horses finished the first lap and disappeared round the bend again.

And it was a proud and happy moment for Jed when, after the race was over, the royal party came down to congratulate Dino on winning the first-ever dinosaur race.

Jed had to lead the animals home once again. He didn't mind. He was very proud and happy. Dino and Sauro had received royal approval, hadn't they? They were becoming more famous every day, weren't they? Never mind what the Parish Clerk had to say about them. He didn't always know when he was well off.

News had spread and all the villagers were out to welcome them home. Jed turned to the Parish Clerk. "I *told* you they would want to see Dino and Sauro. Can't imagine anyone not wanting to. They're the most intelligent and obedient animals in the world."

Afterword

I've always had a problem with dinosaurs. Even the smallest of them, it seems to me, are more than a bit . . . er, *dragonish*. Admittedly, I've known since I was a child that some dinosaurs were really quite shy, many were strictly vegetarian and the whole lot were extinct before there were any human beings on Earth. But suppose *they* didn't know that . . .

Or suppose, by a weird fluke, a few of these strange creatures did survive – on some faraway island, perhaps, or deep in a tropical jungle or (perish the thought) at the bottom of the sort of disused chalk-pit you could find pretty nearly anywhere:

> "Jed couldn't stand it any longer. Getting down on all fours and unheeding the protests of a woman who whacked him with her umbrella, and another who trod on his fingers, he pushed his way through the forest of legs. And there, lying beside the bonfire, was the largest and strangest-looking creature Jed had ever seen.
>
> The beast stirred and Jed, watching wide-eyed, shouted, 'Look! He's waking up.'
>
> The animal slowly lifted up its small head supported on its long neck. Jed could see that a great part of the length of the animal was made up by the very long neck and the very long

tapering tail, with a big body in the middle."

At this point, if I'd been Jed, I'd have got down on all fours again and pushed my way back through the forest of legs as fast as I could go – never mind having my fingers trodden on or being whacked by another umbrella.

Here, though, is where Phyllis Arkle shows what a clever writer she is. Instead of making Jed panic, along with the rest of the crowd, which is almost certainly what would have happened in real life, she imagines the exact opposite. In her version, Jed is excited, the Parish Clerk refuses to believe this creature is a dinosaur at all and Jed's headmaster turns the scene into a sort of nature study lesson. For Dino, amazingly enough, is friendly. And so, when he appears, is Sauro.

Now this alters everything. It means, for instance, that instead of writing some kind of monsters-on-the-rampage saga – however thrilling that might have been – Phyllis Arkle can turn her dinosaurs into heroes. After all, she says, "I've always been fascinated by these lovely, enormous creatures and read as much about them as I could. Often I used to visit the Natural history Museum in London to see the wonderful models and skeletons there. I chose the brontosaurus to write about because this, it seemed to me, was the most famous dinosaur of all." In fact, it's clear from the tales she tells about Dino and Sauro that she expects the reader to become just as fond of them as she is.

And, in the end, aren't we?

Of course, she also wants to make us laugh. "Humour runs in my family," she admits. "I'm not a morose kind of person. I love a good joke." That's why page after page is so hilarious. Some of the jokes are straightforward slapstick – Others concern oddball characters like the Professor or the Parish Clerk (who was based on a real-life person). Funniest of all, for me, is the gag that runs through both books about how two such huge, lumbering creatures can constantly *disappear.* Whatever she's describing, Phyllis Arkle always seems to have a twinkle in her eye and her tongue firmly in her cheek. The word 'droll' could have been invented to sum up her dry, mock-serious tone of voice.

But is that the whole picture, I wonder? Haven't we missed something? I'm thinking of passages like this:

> ". . . As he approached Dino, he saw that the great beast was resting with his head and tail curled round towards his body. Dino raised his head, snuffled a little, and went to sleep again. He didn't object when Jed gave him an approving pat on the top of his head.
>
> Satisfied and with a warm glow in his heart, Jed made his way back to the cottage and climbed wearily up the stairs . . . "

Here it's almost as if Jed were a dad tucking Dino up like a child at bedtime. Behind all the fun and frolics in the *Village Dinosaur* books lies another message, perhaps. Is it what nowadays we'd call a "green" message about looking after endangered species? Or a message about the importance of tolerance and caring for each other, whatever the differences between us?

Maybe it's both.

According to Phyllis Arkle "there's a magic and a mystery about dinosaurs" and by the time we've read these stories we can't help agreeing with her. Mind you, I've still got my doubts about dragons.

Chris Powling

Puffin | Modern | Classics

Some other Young Puffin Modern Classic titles available

THE WORST WITCH
Jill Murphy

MRS PEPPERPOT IN THE MAGIC WOOD
Alf Proyson

CLEVER POLLY AND THE STUPID WOLF
Catherine Storr

ADVENTURES OF THE LITTLE WOODEN HORSE
Ursula Moray Williams

Some other Puffin Modern Classic titles available

BRIDGE TO TERABITHIA
Katherine Paterson

CARRIE'S WAR
Nina Bawden

THE CAY
Theodore Taylor

THE DARK IS RISING
Susan Cooper

THE FOX BUSTERS
Dick King-Smith

Puffin | Modern | Classics

THE MIDNIGHT FOX
Betsy Byars

MRS FRISBY AND THE RATS OF NIMH
Robert O'Brien

ROLL OF THUNDER, HEAR MY CRY
Mildred D. Taylor

THE SILVER SWORD
Ian Serraillier

SMITH
Leon Garfield

STIG OF THE DUMP
Clive King

TARKA THE OTTER
Henry Williamson

THUNDER AND LIGHTNINGS
Jan Mark

TOM'S MIDNIGHT GARDEN
Philippa Pearce

THE TWELFTH DAY OF JULY
Joan Lingard

WATERSHIP DOWN
Richard Adams

A WIZARD OF EARTHSEA
Ursula Le Guin

A WRINKLE IN TIME
Madeleine L'Engle

Puffin | Modern | Classics

ADVENTURES OF THE LITTLE WOODEN HORSE

Ursula Moray Williams

The Little Wooden Horse is Uncle Peder's finest creation, but when no-one wants to buy him, he stays with his master and the two become great friends. When the toymaker grows poor and ill the brave little horse sets out to sell himself.

The Little Wooden Horse has adventures galore whilst trying to make enough money to return to his beloved master.

CLEVER POLLY AND THE STUPID WOLF

Catherine Storr

When Polly opens the door and finds a large black wolf standing on the doorstep waiting to gobble her up, it's the wolf that has the surprise when Polly invites him in.

Clever Polly isn't frightened at all and so begins a series of hilarious adventures as Polly tries to outwit the hungry but inexperienced wolf.

MRS PEPPERPOT IN THE MAGIC WOOD

Alf Prøysen

Mrs Pepperpot never knows when she's going to shrink to the size of her own kitchen pepper-pot, and it's usually at the most inconvenient moments! But she would never have met the little people in the Magic Wood, or been taught to swim by a frog, or ridden on a mouse's back if she had been her normal size.

THE WORST WITCH

Jill Murphy

Mildred Hubble is a trainee witch at Miss Cackle's Academy, and she's making an awful mess of it. She's always getting her spells wrong and she can't even ride a broomstick without crashing it. But she manages to get by until she turns Ethel, the teacher's pet, into her deadly enemy . . .

Carrie's War

Nina Bawden

Evacuated from London to Wales during the Second World War, Carrie and her brother are sent to live with the very strict Mr Evans.

But in trying to heal the breach between Mr Evans and his estranged sister, Carrie does the worst thing she ever did in her life.

The Dark is Rising

Susan Cooper

With only four days until Christmas, plenty of snow outside and his birthday to look forward to, Will has got everything in the world to feel happy about; but he has an overwhelming sense of foreboding.

Suddenly, as everyone else enjoys a normal Christmas, Will is caught up in a powerful and fantastic adventure, battling against the powers of Darkness and evil that threaten to destroy the world.

THE MIDNIGHT FOX

Betsy Byars

Tom lives in the city and he is not looking forward to spending the summer holiday on his uncle's farm.

However, he learns to love the farm when he finds a black fox living in the woods. But his Uncle Fred wants to kill the fox and Tom is determined to help save her.

ROLL OF THUNDER, HEAR MY CRY

Mildred D. Taylor

The Mississippi of the 1930s is a hard place for a black child to grow up in and Cassie finds it difficult to understand why the farm means so much to her father.

But she begins to reach a painful understanding when she witnesses the hatred and destruction around her and learns when it is important to fight for a principle even if it brings terrible hardships.

TARKA THE OTTER

Henry Williamson

This classic story of an otter's life and death in the Devon countryside captures the feel of nature and wildlife as though it is seen through his eyes.

Its atmosphere and detail make it easy to see why Tarka has become one of the best-loved creatures in world literature.

WATERSHIP DOWN

Richard Adams

Fiver felt sure that something terrible was going to happen to the warren – and Fiver's sixth sense was never wrong.

Yet the fleeing band of rabbits could never have imagined the terrors and dangers they were to encounter in their search for a new home.

READ MORE IN PUFFIN

For children of all ages, Puffin represents quality and variety – the very best in publishing today around the world.

For complete information about books available from Puffin – and Penguin – and how to order them, contact us at the appropriate address below. Please note that for copyright reasons the selection of books varies from country to country.

On the world wide web: www.penguin.co.uk

In the United Kingdom: Please write to *Dept. EP, Penguin Books Ltd, Bath Road, Harmondsworth, West Drayton, Middlesex UB7 ODA*

In the United States: Please write to *Consumer Sales, Penguin USA, P.O. Box 999, Dept. 17109, Bergenfield, New Jersey 07621-0120*. VISA and MasterCard holders call 1-800-253-6476 to order Penguin titles

In Canada: Please write to *Penguin Books Canada Ltd, 10 Alcorn Avenue, Suite 300, Toronto, Ontario M4V 3B2*

In Australia: Please write to *Penguin Books Australia Ltd, P.O. Box 257, Ringwood, Victoria 3134*

In New Zealand: Please write to *Penguin Books (NZ) Ltd, Private Bag 102902, North Shore Mail Centre, Auckland 10*

In India: Please write to *Penguin Books India Pvt Ltd, 706 Eros Apartments, 56 Nehru Place, New Delhi 110 019*

In the Netherlands: Please write to *Penguin Books Netherlands bv, Postbus 3507, NL-1001 AH Amsterdam*

In Germany: Please write to *Penguin Books Deutschland GmbH, Metzlerstrasse 26, 60594 Frankfurt am Main*

In Spain: Please write to *Penguin Books S. A., Bravo Murillo 19, 1° B, 28015 Madrid*

In Italy: Please write to *Penguin Italia s.r.l., Via Felice Casati 20, I–20124 Milano*

In France: Please write to *Penguin France S. A., 17 rue Lejeune, F–31000 Toulouse*

In Japan: Please write to *Penguin Books Japan, Ishikiribashi Building, 2–5–4, Suido, Bunkyo-ku, Tokyo 112*

In South Africa: Please write to *Longman Penguin Southern Africa (Pty) Ltd, Private Bag X08, Bertsham 2013*